Unfortunate
Elements
of My
Anatomy

Unfortunate Elements of My Anatomy

Hailey Piper

Illustrated by
Janice Blaine

THE SEVENTH TERRACE

UNFORTUNATE ELEMENTS OF MY ANATOMY
ISBN 13: 978-1-990082-01-6
The Seventh Terrace First Trade Paperback Edition - 2021

The Seventh Terrace
www.the-seventh-terrace.com

To J, destroyer of worlds and foundation of mine.

ELEMENTS

INTRODUCTION

I'll always remember my first Piper. October, 2019, I'd picked up a copy of *The Possession of Natalie Glasgow* on the recommendation of the Ladies of Horror Fiction. Since I found this wonderful cornucopia of amazing new reads, I've struggled to keep up with my "to be read" stack, but *TPONG* didn't languish for long on my shelves. On a night getting close to spooky season, I ran my fingers along the spines of my choices and settled upon the slim volume with the intriguing cover. I love possession stories, but it can be a tough subject to do right. Avoidance of the obvious source material, leading the story on a new path, mapping out fresh ways to turn your reader's blood cold – not a light task to undertake. I'd heard good things, though, so it was with pleasurable anticipation that I ran a bath and settled in for the sliver of me-time I got every day back then.

The first page negated every relaxing property of my bathtub. I don't think I ever even laid back, just sat with my teeth clenched, turning page after page until the water grew cold and I abandoned the tub for the couch. The house was dark and silent, everyone else having long since gone to bed, but I wasn't going anywhere. I was being hunted, the same as Margaret Willow, and there was no way I could rest with the weight of those eyes behind me.

Tension from the first page is what I wrote in my five star review, and it's not hyperbole. "Piper built dread from the first pages, and as everything comes together, it clicks like perfectly matched pieces." I'm quoting myself here because this idea of Hailey's work was prophetic, in a way. As I dove into the search for her words that had come before, perfection became a theme.

Now I'm really sounding hyperbolic. I get that, and yet pondering as I have on how to best express the way it feels to read Hailey Piper, I can't change that impression. I know her work ethic, that she applies herself diligently to writing, that she churns out story after story which serves as its own education. I know, too, that she's a keen and empathetic student of humanity, a supportive and thoughtful friend, and a soft-spoken Amazonian warrior. I know she reads widely, that she edits, and works with editors with whom she graciously shares credit (obligatory shout out to editors everywhere, you wonderful people, you), but whatever the process, what emerges as the completed product feels like a story that was waiting to be told, in precisely the manner in which she spins it on the page. There is always at least one line, and usually many, that feels like a long held truth you've only just heard expressed correctly, that both sings to your life and settles in as a dark reality. For there is no doubt that as you read more, that truth will begin to alter and grow, leaving you to see it in a new light whether you want to or not.

I'm a fan of Hailey's longer fiction – *An Invitation to Darkness* is Gothic horror at its best, and *Benny Rose, the Cannibal King* is both immensely entertaining and the bearer of deeper truths about the role of the young, and specifically girls, and how they're regarded by those that should know better. I'd recommend any of these titles without hesitation, and I can say the same about *Unfortunate Elements of My Anatomy*.

One of the first impressions I had of Hailey's short fiction, and that continues to awe me, is her ability to start her readers on a path just familiar enough to recognize and take the first steps, before branching off into the unknown. This collection travels from the farthest reaches of space, to times long beyond and before our own. To windswept beaches, and high school corridors. To kingdoms and covens that lie just past the borders of our reality, waiting for the right combination of intention and need to open a veil that we, as a reader, know should stay closed. But it is Hailey's gift for empathy that has us parting the veil alongside her characters, even as we flinch away from what is to come. She shows us the ancient dangers of folk horror, the inevitable end in apocalyptic horror, horror which we visit upon ourselves or our loved ones, and that they visit upon us, for the crime of being human and vulnerable. There is horror, too, in the everyday. In bathrooms and bedrooms and vacations, in grocery stores and the very music we make. There is horror in trust, and in love, and in refusing to love. There is tongue in cheek horror and horror in which we cheer the ostensible villains, monsters made infinitely more likable than the humans they hunt. Hailey thinks around corners, and deftly speaks from within the minds of a wide cast of characters. Every point of view she tackles, she sinks deep inside to know their dread and make it ours.

It is a well-known axiom that to understand a genre, it is necessary to study the past masters of it. I don't disagree – there is wisdom to be gained by reading those that came before, but I would posit that it's just as important to read the new ones as well. This is particularly true when it comes to diverse voices. Hailey Piper gives her readers a master class in short fiction, with every tale she writes, and these stories resonate with a wide audience. "Make horror gay AF" is the first line in her Twitter bio, and it's a maxim she lives up to, weaving a strong LGBTQ+ worldview into her work in a successful effort to normalize a life experience that has spent far too long being trampled and marginalized. In so doing, she makes horror *human* AF, including all of us in her skillful prose, and making it impossible to escape what she's about to visit upon us. To that I say, more, please.

One of the many facets that I enjoy about her work I wasn't able to fully articulate until I recently reread Carmen Maria Machado's *The Husband Stitch.* Machado points out with enough clarity for my literal mind to catch what has always bothered me about most urban legends. There is a common undercurrent of warning to them – warnings against being prideful, being poor, being a bride. Even against facing your fears or going on a date. I'll be honest, when I saw those warnings all laid out together, it pissed me off. Which of any of those things is a sin at all, let alone one punishable by death?

The only cautionary theme that runs through Hailey's stories is a dire warning against underestimating the female of the species, and I love it. There is pain here, there are choices that lead to more of it, but as is true in real life, the only way to avoid it is not to be human. Since that's not a possibility for readers or characters, I suggest you settle in and travel the road Hailey shows us. Just don't expect a peaceful ride.

- Laurel Hightower, author of
Whispers in the Dark and *Crossroads*

Feast for Small Pieces

Never underestimate the seductive power of a woman who's minding her own business.

"There's just something about her," they say. I see myself splashed across a pulp magazine cover, a distraught man in the background. The tagline reads, "He met a woman he Could. Not. Resist." As if that's my problem.

These writers don't realize it's me they've placed in their stories. I'd hoped to escape them when I left England, but their tide is unending. They scarce remember passing me on the street, only the fire I've lit in their minds, hearts, and other places. Later they sit with their notebooks or keyboards, tapping out the story of how a man's peaceful life was shattered when he met me in some chance romance.

Sometimes I'm cast as a vampire. Other times I'm the half-human spawn of an elder god. I might be Eve. Never the same, but always me.

Half of these fictional sisters show no interest in men, while others drown in men's wishes. She dressed that way that night knowing she'd rock his world. Her genetics must've known she'd meet him someday and grew her bones and flesh to suit him. We're all so subtly loud in men's eyes.

Feast on a true story.

I visit a grocer to buy tomatoes, plump ones. A man approaches. Were he to write about me, it would be my fault, but the pen is in my hand today. Whether I wear a hoodie two sizes too big with baggy jeans that hide my figure or a skirt that barely passes my waist, it does not matter. I am buying tomatoes.

"Hey, pretty lady. Doing anything tonight?" He shuffles behind me, impatient. "What, you have a boyfriend?"

It's never the same. A compliment, an insult, requests for my name, marital status, smiles, evening plans, swept to sea on tides of apathy.

"If you're single, why not go out with me?"

"Because I don't want to."

Here comes the outrage. Some don't need to be spurned first. Even seeing a woman they like reminds them of their frailty, how their blood is dragged as the moon drags the tide. I don't know them inside, but I've seen what comes out. I'm more fortunate than most. For the woman across the street, this is the moment he beats her or runs her down with his car, anything to destroy her.

His angry words breathe down my neck, all names I've heard before.

I turn, the first time I set eyes on him. "You will leave."

A writer would have slunk away to jot me down as beldam or succubus. A painter might color me an untouchable mother. To a musician, a ballad would pretend we were lovers. They dream of joining me as I dream of leaving them. We live in a world where my fantasy is to buy groceries unmolested.

But this man is no creator. There is no art to him, only crude craving by the responsibility in his pants that I never knew was mine. He would destroy me.

I abandon my shopping today, tomatoes in their basket. "Follow," I say. A stupid part of his brain might believe he's going to get his way.

Killing him would be kind. He would die believing himself like those pulp heroes, a tragic figure who lays his fate at my feet. When they persist, I give them purpose. These men wish I was a vampire, a cosmic demon, a witch. They wish for a clean death.

My workshop is a wooden shed behind my cozy house. By the rustic shingles, sweet green grass, pleasant canary yellow paint, you could never tell what I do there. I keep it insulated, the walls soundproofed. It stinks with heavenly residue. No matter how many airings out I try through its open wooden double doors, the smell remains.

The persistent men never notice. I lead this one inside, where on a wooden workbench I keep my tools shaped from fallen stars, across from the four poster bed. It's soft, comfortable; its guests will spend a great deal of time on it. I order him to strip and then lie down. He's too eager to tear his clothing away and stretch across the crimson sheets.

That isn't the only stripping I need.

Doors closed, I dig my fingers into the workshop wall and tear aside a curtain that blocks this world from the shining heaven few ever notice. In that place, flesh is scarce and sanctified. Even his. Its cosmic perfection pours into his body, makes him ready to be given purpose. My fingers begin the work.

"Lie still," I tell him. His fearful eyes dart this way and that, but he won't get up. It is enough to work with.

There are worthy causes everywhere you look. Here, a woman's vertebrae rub together, causing her daily pain. There, another's skin is missing after a house fire. Blood, hair, eyes, intestines, bones. When I've placed a persistent man in my workshop, I strip what he has, cleanse it in unearthly light, and use it to mend the hurt I see around me. His pieces live on in these healed women, aware. They are pieces put to better purpose than serving him.

A month passes. He is only bone and fragments of skin and muscle. Still aware, still staring from the bed. I need not tell him to lie still anymore; he has no choice. In my neighborhood, a girl falls from a tree and snaps her leg. It could heal with a fracture line, but I make it good as new. Another woman cannot move on after her mother's untimely death. She doesn't know, as I offer her coffee, that it's laced with the strength to find purpose again. She thanks me for the coffee, not the gift from the persistent man.

Everything he was becomes forfeit, even his time, even his will. I waste nothing.

The work finished, I eat what little is left of him. It is only fair after he's put me off supper for weeks. He lives briefly in my digestive track before those remnants, too, are stripped away, become me.

Eventually the women and girls he's helped will grow new cells in their livers and skin, replacing his pieces. He'll fade from the world little by little while the good he's done persists.

Hand that fate to the pulp hero, to the writers, painters, musicians, let them blame me for finding that some men are greater as the division of their parts. I do not shatter lives. They shatter themselves against me, panes of glass thrown at an immovable rock, long weatherworn by rain, eroded slick by frothing waves.

And the tide is unending.

The Law of Conservation
of Death

O n the fifteenth birthday of your third reincarnation, you feel his breath on your skin. New skin, never tainted until now. At once the sky darkens, and balloons, gifts, and cake no longer matter as your lives come rushing back. You've turned fifteen before, but that's the least of it.

He's found you again.

THE FIRST REINCARNATION

Once upon a time, you and he shared a life together. Eventually that life ended. It's a mystery what metaphysical laws dictate who becomes a ghost and who reincarnates, who forgets their past lives and who remembers. You only know his place in the universe and yours.

In this new life, you're born into a family of particular expectations. You're a lady, so act like one. A lady sits quiet and calm. A lady only knows a man's touch when she's married and doesn't fidget as unseen fingers explore her skin.

A lady is not haunted.

You stick with crowds in the daylight, believing the herd will keep you safe from the predator. Conversations muffle his voice. His fleshless fingertips go unfelt when you jostle friends and neighbors on the street.

But at night, you're never as alone as you should be. He enters your chambers and climbs into your bed. A lady mustn't know a man until she's married, but he promises he married you long ago.

You run screaming to your family. They say your wailing is unladylike and accuse you of dreaming. When that excuse is no longer convenient, when you've begun to claw at your skin—how can he touch you if there's no skin?—they accuse you of madness.

At twenty-two years old, you're committed to a madhouse far from home. Your caretakers say they want to help, but you soon learn that "help" is their way of saying "hurt."

No one visits except him. Of course he'll follow wherever you go. He's yours, he says.

There are no crowds to protect you from his whispers, and you feel his fingers until winter numbs your scarred skin. This isolation is familiar. Before you die of pneumonia in your cold asylum cell, you recall the end of that first life in his lonesome castle by the sea.

Where he murdered you.

THE SECOND REINCARNATION

Or tried. A body dies, but it seems life goes on.

You chalk up that last one to bad luck. Surely he can't find you again when the world's population booms between each rebirth. New people surround you, their lives fleeting and precious. The world comes apart as global war looms, but you cling to every fresh sensation.

When his whisper finds you again, you bite your tongue and trim your nails. No one will accuse you of madness this time.

But to keep him secret carries a cost. Quiet surrender makes him comfortable. He calls you by that first name, the one he knew you as in that first life, like it still means something. You tell yourself it's only meaningless syllables.

He wears you down in whispers and strokes. You scream bloody murder and steel yourself for another death in the madhouse. Maybe this time he'll leave you alone.

Fortunately, medical science has advanced since your first reincarnation. They don't diagnose people with madness anymore. This world of needles and electricity and psychology is so civilized. You aren't mad; you have a condition. Most women have those, don't they? Perfectly treatable. Take two pills every evening and get some rest.

Nice as it is not to die in a cold cell, there's no treatment for haunting. If you and he were married, death should have parted you, yet he persists. Is your tethering his doing? Did he somehow bind you together after that first life? He never talks about what happened between murdering you and haunting you. He only says that he's yours, that he won't stop being yours so long as there's a you to have him. He knows nothing about the laws of death. Not that he would try to learn; he's so single-minded. Ghosts are obsessed with the past.

Not you. Each life is a new experience. There are people you care about, people you despise, and they have births and weddings and deaths. What becomes of them? Reincarnation? Ghosts? A fabled something else? None of them haunt you. Only him.

You bear out this second reincarnation long as you can, first surrounded by loved ones, and then alone in tears and hatred.

He never leaves. If there's something he wants, you don't know what it is, and you wouldn't give it to him if you did. Maybe this time, since you haven't died young, you'll escape him. Your cells decay faster than your body can make them, and you dream of wasting away in flakes too tiny for his grasping fingers to put you back together.

Death comes for your heart in the night while his breath strokes your white hair.

THE THIRD REINCARNATION

Third time's the charm, right?

He's absent when you come into consciousness, but that's nothing new. A child again, you teach new legs to walk and learn a new world of computers and gizmos. You turn eight, nine, ten. By now, you've usually heard his voice, felt his breath or fingers, but there's nothing. He must have lost you this time.

You believe it up until your fifteenth birthday. Your friends and family sing over birthday cake, but when they say your new name, his whisper tickles your ear with the old one. You blow out the candles and can't tell if they sputter under your breath or his.

This family is wealthy, and money brings temporary freedom. When you make up reasons to abandon home, they move. Every new town is a kind of reincarnation—new friends, new memories, and a brief reprieve from him.

But each time, he finds you. Maybe not as fast as he lets on, but his obsession whispers at sleepovers, school dances, and first dates. He can't help himself. He's yours, the possession you never wanted. Time to move again.

Running gets tiresome, especially once you're grown and have to arrange the move yourself. Everywhere you go, you hunt down religious leaders and spiritual gurus who try every blessing and exorcism known to man. Their rituals are hollow comfort. Nothing dispels him.

Not even love.

You meet someone else. He's kind and adventurous, knows how to shake a laugh out of you even on your worst days, and that means something. You let your guard down and marry him. He doesn't mind moving every few months and never treats you like a burden. He says he'll do anything for you.

But he also says he's yours, and you can't call it romantic. The sentiment's been tainted since long before he was born. When those words are whispered at night, you can't always tell who speaks them. Are there two in your bed, or three? Across decades and deaths you've learned that "I'm yours" is the ghost's way of saying "You're mine." He isn't even jealous of the new marriage. Life ends, but you and he are forever.

You divorce your wonderful husband and flee again, perhaps for the last time. There's a seaside town reputed for hauntings where people come to meet lost loves and let go. You hope the abundant spiritual traffic will make his road difficult.

But still he finds you. He always does.

He wears you down again until you're inspired by your first reincarnation to grow out your nails and tear yourself to pieces. It's the most you can do. You're too tired to run anymore.

Tonight you stare out your beach house window, the big one that faces the sea, while raw red scratches bleed down your arms. His nostalgic breath fogs the glass as he again reminisces over that first life. Don't you recall listening to the waves then, too? You were happy, he says.

You remember differently. Yes, there was a seaside castle, ancient long before you were born. You would want for nothing there if only you found contentment between its walls and turned a blind eye to your personal Bluebeard and his bloody secret rooms. Not to worry, he said. You weren't like the others. You were special, and he would keep you.

Foolish girl, you believed him! You were actually surprised when he came in the night to hurt you in a new way.

Standing at the beach house window, you realize those are your earliest memories. There's nothing before the castle, time having turned all prior relationships to dust. How can you even be sure that life was first? You might have lived a thousand forgotten lives until you met him. Why does this one stay? The murder? He can't be the only one who's murdered you before; you're not that likable.

And what next?

Your fourth reincarnation might birth you in a digital age, where consciousness rockets through virtual worlds. And he'd find you. You know he would. It wouldn't matter what chips they put in your brain or tubes they insert in your nervous system. He would be there, breathing on your skin and whispering a name that won't die. Your fifth reincarnation? That might take you to space or another planet. He would reach you even there, tethered across the stars.

And if this world comes crashing down instead, he would thrive. Every moment would be a struggle between baking skies and boiling seas, the saltwater fauna having turned as single-celled and all-consuming as their Precambrian ancestors. In your desperate misery, you'll at last reach for him and submit. Yes, he's yours. Yes, you're his.

Purple-orange sunset overtakes the window. He presses ghostly arms around you and whispers old promises. Had he flesh, he would crush your body. Instead, he crushes your soul.

You leave his touch and step out the door. Neighboring beach houses lean in to watch with lightless eyes, gossipy as their occupants. It's one of those nights you can't be sure you're coming back. Maybe there's one last run in you after all.

Across from the houses, the ocean curls foamy, inviting fingers. You could hit that beach and keep on walking. People have said that, haven't they? That they'll walk into the ocean. They mean drowning, but death isn't enough for you. There would still be a you, and so long as there's a you, he'll say he's yours.

Your nails tear your clothes away in the coastal wind. You're naked as you approach the sea, but not naked enough. There's still skin, the same you've clawed at across lifetimes to escape his fingers. Your nails burrow into it, freeing yourself in bloody strips, until at last you've torn your skin away and can crawl raw on the sand. Freed flesh turns porous as you slap through the surf, where saltwater seeps into your amphibious new form. Wading into the tide, your limbs turn soppy, scales coat your hide, and your skull splits and reshapes so your eyes can migrate to each side of your head. In the depths, you become a fish that has walked back into the ocean.

But de-evolution isn't the end. You must degenerate. You must divide into scattered pieces. Not a ghost, not reincarnation, but that fabled something else.

It isn't enough to die. You must be unmade.

The ocean rips at your scales, blood, bones, brain. Every organ segregates into homogenous cell swarms. Then the cells scatter, becoming solitary creatures, each having decided that being part of a complex organism isn't a future they want.

Better that each becomes a lonesome amoeba. Better to carve out a Precambrian existence in the modern world than to know another moment of him.

He finds you in the last moments as your cells disperse forever. Leaving empty footprints in the sand, he approaches the water's edge and whispers the old name, but now it really is only meaningless syllables. Is it even a sound when there's no one to hear? His grasping fingers stroke the shredded skin you've left behind, but he can't put you back together. There are only scraps, and memories, and the lonely eternity that awaits him.

There is no you to haunt.

Demons of Particular Taste

O n Halloween night, Lin lay tied to her bed, beyond ready to get this thing out of her.

Black candles mounted her dim bedroom's every dresser and nightstand. Their fires flickered in Kristie's eyes as she arose from behind the footboard, having finished Lin's last knots.

"Is this necessary?" Lin tugged an outstretched arm. The rope went taut from the bedpost.

"Exorcisms aren't gentle," Kristie said, climbing onto the bed with a book in hand. "You wouldn't want the expulsion to damage the body." She sounded strange, saying that.

Not that Lin was one to talk. An alien roar surged up her throat. "*Waiting is bogus. Get with the tubular waves.*" The demon was eager to see this fail.

Lin couldn't let it. "I'm ready."

Kristie straddled Lin's chest and raised the book high. "On this night, when the veil is thin, I call upon the powers of the heavens and the earth."

Lin closed her eyes. The weight made her light-headed, not unlike the demon's first coming. Everyone knew to keep clear of Ouija boards, but Skip-It? No warning there. She'd found the mangled purple plastic toy at a yard sale and wanted to make a silly video. Its electronic noises came crackled and warped, but she'd chalked that up to deterioration. She couldn't have guessed this Skip-It held a demon until she slipped its purple loop around her ankle and blacked out.

A growl in her throat woke her after. Nexistopheles had moved in.

After that came every exorcism movie cliché—crawling on walls, speaking in tongues, twisting men's genitals, and so on.

Worst was worrying over Kristie. They had been dating four years, ever since Kristie's dad kicked her out, but their relationship had been on the rocks this past year. Kristie always seemed bored and nothing Lin tried could re-stoke their fires. The last thing they needed was demonic possession, and having Nexistopheles share their bed had turned innocent cuddling into Russian roulette. Brave Kristie slept each night without knowing whether she'd awaken to her girlfriend or the demon.

But she was here and helping. "Let open the depths," she said, legs squeezing Lin's sides, almost reassuring. "Let them feast. Leave one soul to this body and drag Lin's presence to the royal pits of darkness."

Lin's eyes flashed open. "Whose?" She regarded Kristie's stoic expression and the book in her hand. That was no King James Bible.

It was Lin's diary.

She yanked at the ropes again. "The hell?"

Kristie grimaced at the diary. "I'd normally never violate your privacy, but she said I needed remnants of your soul to press you out."

Unpleasant thoughts linked together quick. "You're helping the demon?"

Kristie shrugged. "Nothing personal. You aren't terrible, but you aren't Nexi."

"I'm your girlfriend!"

"My boring girlfriend. You pretend you're quirky with your yard sale dives and dumb videos, but they're window dressing for a dull personality. And that'd be fine, every social ladder needs a bottom rung—"

"A *what?*"

"—but Nexi does actual cool things. Last week, she manifested me a new phone. Yesterday she made my dad's car explode."

Lin's vision swam. "I don't remember."

"You were inactive." Kristie sighed, bored again already. "Point is, I got a chance to trade up, and who wouldn't take that?"

Lin wriggled. "I wouldn't!"

"Whatever. You ready, Nexi?"

"*Cowabunga*," Nexistopheles growled.

To think there might've been a chance for them. Instead, Lin was the candy wrapper around a sugary demonic prize. Did she mean anything to Kristie? Did anyone? Lin didn't think so. Her heart hollowed as the ropes tightened.

Kristie raised the diary overhead. "I cast you out, Lin Moreau. Leave this vessel and never return!" She slammed the diary against Lin's chest.

The bed gave way beneath Lin's soul. She wasn't falling yet, but her spiritual fingers clung to an uncertain precipice. From beneath came the stares of dead family, everyone she'd escaped long ago, now waiting with open arms in the worst way.

"Hang on!" Lin shouted. "We can work this out."

"Hey, bargaining." Kristie smirked. "That's the fourth stage of grief, right?"

Lin's jaw snapped open. "*Math's for nerds. Toss her out of my body, girlfriend.*" She swallowed the demon's voice. "It's my body!"

"It's a body." Kristie raised the diary again. "Possession is nine-tenths of the law. Especially in Hell."

A body. That's right; Kristie had sounded strange saying *the* body. Lin wouldn't want to damage it.

Or would she?

Before the diary slammed down again, she put her chin to chest and banged her skull against the wooden headboard. She kept banging as she pressed one forefinger back on the bedspread and rammed her hand down, breaking the digit. The ropes resisted, but she yanked one arm so hard that her wrist snapped with a wet crack. Pain burst through her bones.

The demon felt everything. "*Stop her,*" Nexistopheles said, but Lin bit her tongue until blood filled her mouth.

Kristie sat stiff on Lin's chest, wide-eyed and useless.

Nexistopheles spoke again, but not from Lin's throat. The voice hung in the air. "*If this lame body's gonna wipe out that fast, I don't want it no more.*" A jolt quaked Lin's spine as the demon dove through the bed, shrieking and laughing until she was far below earshot.

Kristie tossed the diary and clambered up Lin's trunk, cupping hands around her cheeks. "Nexi, don't go! The body will heal and then we'll be radical or whatever."

Lin spat blood at Kristie's eyes. "She's gone."

Kristie slunk back. She didn't bother to wipe the blood off her face. "Oh."

The room grew quiet except for Lin's strained breath and the silent screams of her broken finger and wrist. She waited for the fresh hollowness in heart to fill when she looked to

Kristie, but it had turned cold, like it wasn't her heart anymore. Just some heart she happened to have inside her that kept beating despite betrayal.

"Kristie?"

"Mm?"

"Fucking untie me."

I'm Not a Chainsaw Kind of Girl, But…

T he heart wants what it wants. You might say that justified my friends' relationships, but sometimes the best people settle for less. My heart wanted their freedom from these walking trashcans.

"But Zoe, if they love them, you have to love them." Hell with that.

Daphne's boyfriend was Chad. A fun pastime for hulking, breath-of-death Chad was hitting on the waitresses at Daphne's favorite diner, Ribbed for Her Pleasure, while she sulked beside him. Have you ever seen the light leave a happy person's eyes? One minute, she's a bubbly explosion of sunshine, the next he steps into the room and fills her up with shadow. All it takes is his presence. Her voice shrinks; her eyes dim. The sunshine's gone.

After a while, you get sick of the eclipse.

And then there was Lucille's boyfriend Gary, who traded personality for I Can't Believe It's Not Personality. He liked to shout, "Women's March—into the kitchen!" with a laugh whenever she'd see him after her business meetings. How'd they get together? No idea, but if I let them keep dating, I'd only see Lucille during Fishkill Correctional visiting hours after she murdered him.

Murder. Now there was an idea.

But I didn't want to get my hands dirty. Thankfully there were means even for the immaculate fingers of piano players like me.

I hosted at my place, Daphne, Lucille, and the riffraff. What furniture I brought home came unwanted from the ends of driveways. Wall paintings were gifts. I gathered the books from dime sales. Clean, comfortable, a nice, lonesome house by the woods without nice things inside it.

Except my piano.

That silvery Steinway soaked up every spare dollar, and I never regretted it. Each thrumming piano wire brought solace to lonely evenings. She drove Daphne, Lucille, and I to brighter moods. I could fill my house with people, but her simplest melody would silence the room.

You might call it sacrilege to bring the likes of Chad and Gary where they might rest their beer cans on her perfect lid. They had precious few chances to do so. I kept myself busy dusting her while waiting for someone to make an inevitable discovery.

"This the last can?" Chad asked, incredulous. "You got a six-pack for five people?"

Gary snickered. "At her majesty's palace, everyone's the designated driver."

I flicked on the outside light, casting orange into the dark across my tiny toolshed, gravel driveway, and Chad's rust-colored pick-up beside my little red sedan. "Sounds like you two just volunteered for the beer run."

Chad slammed his first and last beer can onto my glass coffee table. Beads of condensation counted seconds as he grabbed his and Gary's coats. "Coming, baby?"

Daphne looked to him and then to me. She was water; Lucille was smoke. They would change shape to fit whatever vessels the men stored them in, and those vessels shrank by the week.

"We'll stay," I said. "Let our knights in shining armor deliver refreshments."

They grinned, Gary bowed, and they left. Chad's truck roared alive, honked twice, and scattered gravel as it pounced onto Laird Road.

Daphne picked up Chad's beer can and rattled remaining drops onto her tongue. Her light came crawling back. Lucille went on seething until she lit a cigarette.

I scoffed at the door. "I'm on a diet from men. No more boyfriends."

"What about a girlfriend?" Daphne asked. "Who was that orchestra sweetie you used to see?"

I shrugged, remembering Celine the harpsichordist. "No more girlfriends, either. At least with boys, I know the fallout isn't my fault. If I split with a woman, I'll probably be who's to blame.

Smoke snaked through Lucille's lips. "We feed our hearts the pieces of animals that other people throw away."

Daphne doubled over, giggling.

Had the men never been there, it might have been an ordinary Friday night, but shadows clawed at my girls' expressions. I tried not to be giddy at this being the final time. My head had to be clear for playing the piano, both with the men gone and after they returned.

The piece came from a borrowed library text, *Concerto Ombra*. Never heard of it? When seeking forbidden tomes and their power, most would prefer your average *Necronomicon*. Few would suspect a collection of sheet music to hold otherworldly gifts. Nothing worth your attention, unless you can read the music. The original book was supposedly scrawled by eighteenth century Italian composers using ink infused with the ashes of burned Wicked Bibles. They later tore out their eyes for unknown reasons. That copy wasn't available via interlibrary loan.

Resting the book on the piano's music shelf, its pages held open by hair clips, I played "Gemini Sonata to Instill." It began with flirtatious high notes before making a slow descent into minor keys.

Daphne and Lucille swept to either side of the Steinway. Curls bounced with Daphne's head as she bobbled along to the melody. She was already attuned.

Lucille's smoke danced when she spoke. "It's gorgeous."

Practice had meant playing the song's sections out of order. Maddening, but I couldn't risk stitching the piece from beginning to end before the night my friends took their places beside my piano.

"Lucille, could you turn toward me? Perfect. Daphne, slide to the left. Yes, beautiful." I smiled at them. Nearing the finale, my hands stretched to both ends of the keys. "My muses. I love you both so much."

Maybe it was my contrast to their boyfriends' attitudes, maybe the music, but tears glittered in Daphne's eyes. Lucille clasped her hands around her dying cigarette. "Aw, Zoe." They had heard me play a lot of songs on my piano, but this one they took to heart. This they felt was theirs.

They could not have been more right.

I swung both hands down in a discordant clang. The reverberating piano wire ate through my blood vessels into my bursting chest. Was this how heart attacks felt? I had never cast a spell before and didn't know what to expect. My friends must've felt it worse. Their limbs straightened to either side, every muscle taut. Lucille's cigarette butt hit her shoe and spat frail embers onto my carpet.

At last they were no longer malleable substances reshaped by other vessels but had become solid vessels themselves.

Pain eased as the final note's echoes melted. I was myself again, but Daphne and Lucille cricked their necks and joints as if adjusting to bones and flesh. Muscles knotted beneath Lucille's skin, and her eyes lit with a cigarette's glow. She stalked closer, a tiger in lady's clothing.

"Behave yourself," a sweet voice breathed through Daphne's lips. Her wrists crossed daintily under her belly. "You're threatening our Conjurer, and that's a no-no."

My brain stalled. Part of me hadn't believed this would work, yet here were two things that wore my best friends' faces. Things I had brought into the world.

Daphne's finger traced the Steinway lid. "Does the Conjurer have a name?"

"No," I coughed out. "How does this work? You grant me a wish and each take cuts of my soul?"

"You have no soul to give. You are a soul. You have a body, and we'll take pieces of it. For me, your eyes."

Something that wasn't Lucille growled through her throat.

"She wants your left foot." Daphne's head tilted. "Just pieces, Conjurer. Pieces in exchange for a boon. Then we'll take your flesh and be on our way."

"And leave the vessels unharmed."

"Absolutely. How else could we someday use them again?" Daphne's eyes glittered, still wet with tears. She couldn't experience this, could she? *Concerto Ombra* suggested the vessels would feel nothing, but that could mean many things. "How can we please you, Conjurer?"

I had to word this just right. "I've summoned you into these women to make them break up with their boyfriends. Permanently."

The demons glanced at each other as if there was something weird about my request and then turned back with clumsy grins, unused to lips and teeth. One look said Daphne and Lucille weren't in the driver's seats. That transparency made me feel a little better about taking their agency even for their own good.

Headlights washed the picture window. The men were back.

"Do we have an understanding?" Daphne asked.

I stammered out an agreement as gravel scraped the soles of boots. Gary burst through the door, an open beer can in each hand. "Your heroes have returned!" Frothing yellow waterfalls drained across his waiting mouth and piddled onto my carpet. Chad bumped him inside, carrying two can-stuffed grocery bags.

I grabbed Daphne's fever hot shoulder and guided her toward Chad.

Her arms wrapped around his neck as he set the bags down. "Honey, isn't there somewhere private we can go? I want to reward my hero."

Chad grinned like he'd expected this greeting and nodded toward his truck. He led Daphne outside.

She stopped him at the hood, head craning toward my toolshed. "In there."

Chad didn't look my way for permission, only followed.

Gary kicked the door shut and leered at Lucille. "Hey, is only one hero getting rewarded around here?"

Lucille's growl melted into a purr as she sauntered to Gary and pressed against his chest.

"Shucks, it weren't nothing, princess." His legs wobbled, threatened to throw him into the mess he'd made.

They must have continued drinking on the way back. Gary should've noticed that Lucille wasn't irritated by his nonsense. Chad wasn't bewildered by Daphne's sudden forwardness. Did they know my friends at all?

Pearls before swine. Violence isn't the answer, but it can be the vague detour you take through a midterm essay to finagle a passing grade.

Lucille's lips found Gary's, locked over them. I watched their jaws at work, his cheek bulging where her tongue explored inside. Chest swelling, her teeth withdrew from his lips, steam rising across her tongue.

He grabbed his throat, eyes wide. She smoked him like the cheap cigarette he was and let him fall to the floor with the other cigarette's remains. I didn't check his neck for a pulse. The demon inside Lucille had finished him.

Was Daphne doing the same to Chad in my toolshed?

A chainsaw's roar answered, and then a scream I gauged at a high C4. The screaming stopped short, but the chainsaw went on grinding. I made myself listen, pictured what Daphne was doing to Chad. Part of my price. There was no going back.

When at last the chainsaw quieted, Daphne opened the door. Blood spattered her skin and clothes and dripped into the carpet's beer puddle.

I slid around my piano toward the linen closet. "Chad's dead?"

"Dead beyond dead," she said.

I tossed a towel at her. This was real. I collapsed onto the piano seat, hand against my forehead. Chad and Gary, dead beyond dead.

Lucille grumbled. Daphne wiped her face and cleared her throat. "Time for payment, Conjurer."

"Right." I rubbed my eyes as if that would make losing them any easier. "One left foot, two eyes, and you both leave my friends unharmed."

"That is the arrangement."

I had a different arrangement in mind and turned to its page of *Concerto Ombra*. My fingers danced the keys quicker this time, better practiced than the last piece.

Thankfully, the song was shorter. Those Italian composers knew it would need to be played in a hurry.

"Let's skip to that last step." My hands hammered the final notes for "Ode to Minor Dismissal." This time, the spell didn't hurt me.

Daphne and Lucille stiffened like before and then crumpled beside Gary. I didn't see the demons leave their bodies, but their skin became lukewarm to touch. They were free, demons and boyfriends exorcised.

Everything had gone as planned. Daphne's joyride with the chainsaw was unexpected, but I was used to cleaning up other people's messes.

First I tended to my friends, hauling Lucille onto the couch and then Daphne beside her. I would drag Gary outside and check the damage on Chad, maybe burn down the toolshed if necessary. No one would find the bodies. The woods were lousy with places for nature to wipe a corpse from the world. I turned to Gary.

A line of light cut through the slightly open front door across the beer-soaked carpet. Gary was gone. Had Lucille only dazed him?

Outside, an engine revved alive. Footsteps tramped the gravel, metal teeth growling toward my front door. A shadow cut the line of light from the carpet just as Gary burst through, the chainsaw grinding between his hands. Sinewy tissue stretched across his cracking skull. Each side of his head was scrambling to escape the other.

I stood stunned in front of the sofa, my coffee table and tender flesh the only defenses between the chainsaw and my friends.

"I'll have those eyes now," Gary said out the left side of his mouth. His right cheek tore open, where new, sharp teeth hissed through the wound. "And she'll have that foot. You cheated us, and that's a no-no."

There was a song to fix this, right? I dodged behind the piano and leafed through *Concerto Ombra*. Why had I kept that chainsaw? I'd used it once on a tree that leaned too close to the house, and it had sat unused in my toolshed ever since.

Those neglected metal teeth tore vengeance into the back of my Steinway. Gary's head split deeper down the middle, and his arms split at the elbows, giving him four narrow arms. His right side was desperate to crawl across the piano lid. Given time, the bones and tissue would mold and reform his body into two vessels of the demons' liking.

I flipped pages. "Galassia Crescendo," "Aria of Solar Silence."

They must have realized I would find an arrangement to stop them. All hands ditched the chainsaw where it had chewed itself into my piano, and double-possessed Gary scrambled after me. I toppled over the piano seat with the book and circled to the dormant chainsaw.

Why didn't each demon possess one of the men? Because Chad was sawed to pieces? A broken vessel gave little to control, hence Gary's tedious mitosis rather than being torn asunder in one breath. I wriggled the chainsaw free from the wood. Teeth had not touched piano wire. I'm not sure which would have broken, but the chainsaw was certainly stronger than flesh. I tugged its chain, and it rumbled to angry life just as Gary reached me.

The demons' coordination was sloppy. They couldn't stop themselves.

Hot blood spewed into my hair, clothes, and mouth. One rip down the middle was all it took—the double-possessed body flopped onto the floor. Tendons scrabbled after each other to mend, but they needed time. I wouldn't give it to them. I sawed across every limb and joint until Gary was a mangled mess of harmless parts.

The things I do for friendship.

I would have to take Daphne and Lucille to their apartment before cleaning. Come home, drag the pieces into linens, bind them in cord, fetch Chad's remains. Replace carpet. Mend piano. So much work, but I would make everything perfect. For real this time.

Except dismemberment hadn't exorcised the demons. Gary's chunks twitched, his tubes sloshing like blind snakes. One demon moaned. I could bury the pieces, but someday they might come back.

My friends deserved freedom. Anything less just wasn't good enough.

I washed my hands until the water ran clear. Enough blood had rained across my Steinway's silvery lid. I wouldn't blemish her keys with red fingerprints.

"Nocturne of Major Dismissal." I hadn't practiced this one, but there was no musical piece I couldn't conquer. My cautious fingers crept across the keys with flawless precision from first note to last. My nerves eased, and the demonic moan faded. The room was silent.

All conjuring was complete. Only the long night of hard labor remained.

But before I stood, another piano began to play. It was a pleasant, somber tune. I scrutinized my fingers as if they would play on their own, but my hands rested on the lap of my bloodstained jeans.

Someone else was playing.

To my left, my friends sat unconscious on the sofa. To my right, dark glass reflected a negative of my living room. At my Steinway's reflection, there sat the Piano Man.

His piano inverted mine, black wood, black keys under white. A fitted tuxedo dressed his long limbs, and white gloves covered his spindly fingers. I couldn't see his face; he wore a curling mask over his head shaped like a black teardrop. Maybe that was his head.

My living room wasn't large, but he looked to sit a thousand feet away while also right beside me. The wind tugged at me as if a door had been opened on a stormy day.

"Who are you?" I asked.

"You have already named me." His voice thrummed in a discordant octave. "The Piano Man."

I slipped through the black window's veil into the monochrome reflection of my home. The floor felt uncertain, as if the gusty room was being drawn through a breath. "Which song is this?"

"It has no name, lest you give it one. You're fond of names." He seemed different from the demons. They were cats, teasing and predatory. The Piano Man was unlike any animal, any person, more a sucking breath where a living thing might be. Like he was nothing at all. "There are darker things than demons, from darker places than their pit."

He grew more distant at every step. My face's reflection curved across his teardrop face. "I take it you don't want my soul either."

"Where I come from, we don't believe in souls. You desire dismissal. I am here to dismiss."

The wind ripped at my blood-soaked clothes. We were being smoked, same as Gary, to be exhaled somewhere that the black window would darken the sun.

"Peculiar analogies occur to you." The Piano Man's notes slipped tears from my eyes.

I had never considered there might be another pianist on the far side of the music. I had to reach him, overtake his song of doom.

"What else can we conjure from you?" he hummed.

Bad that he knew my thoughts, worse that he played them back at me. Teary-eyed, I focused on his piano across the onyx floor. It became the boom box across my childhood den, its cassette silenced so my parents could shout at each other, prelude to their divorce. Its lid became my mom's house, running from my car's back windshield the day I left her. It morphed into my ex's car on the rainy night he wouldn't drive me back from town unless I stretched across his back seat. That was a long walk home.

The Piano Man cocked his head to one side. "You have such grim songs."

Soaked, shaking, I had to approach these things I never wanted to touch again. It was the only way. I reached the piano's backside and grasped its polished wood to steady my legs. Some pieces of this place were brought by him, others by me. A ragged gash bared his piano wires, the lid chewed open by grinding metal teeth.

A monochrome chainsaw rested below, a shadow to mine. I picked it up, fought the distance to the piano bench, and yanked the chain. It growled at the Piano Man's teardrop.

His gloved fingers went on tinkling the keys. "After you kill me, what will you do? You cannot take back notes once played. 'Nocturne of Absolute Dissolution' then? The void may open to drink this mirror, but whose thirst will it quench?"

"If the song's finished, why haven't you stopped playing?" I asked.

He didn't answer me, but I think, somewhere in my reflection, he smiled.

I drove the chainsaw across his teardrop. It cried oil over the piano, but it wasn't mine and I didn't care about its sanctity. He hit the floor in silence.

The piano welcomed me to sit in his place. I laid the chainsaw beside me. The music was carved into the desk of the music shelf, the only song meant to be played here. I could run back through the window, grab *Concerto Ombra*, and play "Nocturne of Absolute Dissolution" like the Piano Man suggested. I could conjure again.

But every note I'd played had made the night worse, a simple beer run turned into a rocket ride to hell and beyond. This black window would lead to bad things. An opened void, a mysterious presence within? That could be worse. Maybe I had to let things be less than perfect, just this once, for the sake of humanity.

Even if it meant the end for me.

I rested my fingers on the piano's black keys. The Piano Man's blood slid across and between them, but wouldn't have a chance to congeal as the wind took on hurricane might.

There was time for one more song. I pressed into the gentle, strolling notes of Scarlatti's "Sonata in F Minor," the kind of piece you can't find in *Concerto Ombra*. It can be played with intensity, but that wasn't my way. I wanted a calm score to the big exhalation. Scarlatti led my thoughts to kinder places than the Piano Man had shown me. I'd never played so well.

The black window collapsed, all molecules breathed in a single, clapping note. I think it was a D sharp.

I can't believe I lived.

Consciousness found me at early dawn lying in the grass between the woods and where my house used to be. Furniture lay strewn in pieces no bigger than my driveway's gravel. The toolshed was obliterated. I pulled myself up from beneath the severed hood of Chad's truck, right wrist cut at the ulna, left hand mangled. I might play piano again, but never like before.

My sofa was spared. Daphne and Lucille weren't much worse for wear. They collapsed beside me in the grass, bewildered at what had changed since they passed out, Daphne drinking, Lucille smoking. I helped them with that.

"Thought Chad was here," Lucille said. "And Gary."

Smoke billowed from my mouth. "The night's kind of a blur. I'm sure they're around."

"Just like that weasel to scurry off when I was finally going to drop him."

Daphne snorted laughter. "Weird. I was going to end it with Chad."

I didn't say anything. Arms tucked to my chest, I looked toward Laird Road, down which I would usually enjoy an unobstructed view of the sunrise across green hills.

A gargantuan black pyramid sucked at dawn's maroon horizon. Sunlight's fingers played notes across its surface. Daphne nestled her head on my shoulder, Lucille curled her knees to her chest, and together we listened to the morose melody that played between sky and nothingness. Evidence of my misdeeds was buried by the almost-apocalypse I had caused. If you ever need to cover a crime, keep that in your back pocket.

My piano was broken into a thousand pieces, but my chainsaw sat intact nearby, her shadow departed with the rest of the black window. We stopped the Piano Man's song before it reached its crescendo. The black pyramid's presence isn't perfect, but I promise, it could've been worse. And it might've cost more to undo. I'll take a lost piano over that.

I'm not a chainsaw kind of girl, but her teeth sure are pretty when they catch the sunshine.

Candyland

ere they came, the high school princesses.
Catherine pressed flat against her locker to let
them stride past. No two were exactly alike, but
each sported luxurious hair, designer outfits, and jewelry
that shined from top to toe. Their gravity sucked Catherine
closer, all the years they wouldn't live having fed the power
of the few they would.

One princess was old enough to drive, but her benefactor
collected her with the others anyway. It was a chance for her
to show off his limousine, her status. The princesses only
attended school when they felt like gossiping with common
girls, who got the chance to see aristocrats when they came
to pick up their charges. As the princesses passed, onlookers
sprayed cheap perfume at their necks. One more period until
school's end.

Catherine's friends scoffed beside her. "Wannabes," Emily said. "Like they can't find anything better to do with their lives."

Bethany nodded. "They'll never be sweet."

Catherine watched the princesses' glittering fingers and glanced at her bare hands. She liked seeing their aristocrats, though none of theirs were her favorites whose names she'd written through her notebook and encircled with hearts— Lawrence Kennedy, Maratha Abdel, Sir Hensley DuPont.

The last had just arrived in America this week. He'd finished off his most recent princess a month back and was scouting for another. Every common girl dreamed it would be her.

Especially Catherine. "Got to go."

She scuttled from the hall into a restroom stall and plopped her bag on her lap. Bottles stared from inside, filled with scented oils and free perfume samples. She lathered her hands and rubbed her neck, underarms, and sides. Some oils stung—an allergy, maybe—but she chanted herself through it.

"Show no pain. They wouldn't like pain. Be delicious."

Any discomfort was worth a chance at aristocratic attention. She didn't care what they really were; they looked human and were far more mature and attractive than greasy boys her age. Sir Hensley's sharp cheek bones, rugged black goatee, and chilly blue eyes were the stuff of dreams.

She wanted to at least make a good impression on his fellows. Everyone said she was pretty, not gaunt like Emily or lopsidedly awkward like Bethany, but aristocrats didn't care about looks. They wanted sweets.

One could start eating his princess at any moment, but chose to savor her presence the way he would later savor her taste. How exciting that had to be. Catherine imagined sitting with Sir Hensley, letting his firm yet gentle hands brush her hair, tension quaking between them at every stroke. He'd want to reveal hidden tongues and devour her, but not yet! She wouldn't be ripe yet. Wanted but unattainable. Just the thought hatched playful butterflies in her stomach.

"Be delicious, just be—"

She hushed when the restroom door opened. Muffled chatter passed the stall to the mirrors, where her friends paused to fix their makeup.

"You're sure?" Emily asked.

"It's what I heard," Bethany said. "Liverpool on Monday, Manhattan yesterday, here today. Hensley's scouting for new prospects."

Catherine shivered. Sir Hensley? Coming here today? Her selected oils took on sudden importance.

Emily clicked her tongue. "Browse the menu, you mean."

"It's a bloodline thing." Bethany made puckering noises. "Total elitist racism."

"It's like, 'oh, you're rich and immortal? Then please, help yourselves to our daughters.' Sickos."

"They should burn." The girls zipped their purses and left the restroom.

Sour grapes, that's all they meant. Every girl daydreamed she might someday be a princess. Sir Hensley was coming. He'd stand on the same tiled floor as Catherine and her friends, but she was the one he would uplift to teenage glory.

Oh, who was she kidding? She would be fifteen next year, too old for any aristocrat's liking. Princesses that age were already being reared as future sweets. Catherine's life was passing her by. It would never be her.

But couldn't it be? She rubbed her skin with renewed ferocity before heading to class.

The final period dragged toward school's end. She couldn't keep her thoughts on biochemistry when every second brought Sir Hensley closer, with his dark hair, crimson suits, and piercing gaze. Phone hidden on her lap, Catherine reread bookmarked articles on what made a girl most likely to be chosen.

Usually they came from large families to ensure there would always be plenty of humans to breed. That was one knock against Catherine; all she had was her little brother.

But a bigger knock was flavor.

"On coming to our world," one article said, "aristocrats discovered their special appendages turned human flesh into sweet substances similar to licorice, hard candy, and so on, which they enjoy. Experts agree that aristocrats harvest the best candy from girls under nineteen. Fed special diets, adolescent girls can be groomed to each man's taste until they're of proper age to be consumed. The process of candying a human, as with applying perfume, draws out the individual's natural flavor. Delicious human, delicious candy. Bland human—"

That was Catherine in a nutshell. Bland. The article might as well have displayed her school photo.

The last bell buzzed. Catherine darted out of class as the princesses again strode past, nearly ramming into them. She scurried behind, keeping in step. No one else would reach the aristocrats first.

There they stood at the school's west exit. Catherine's heart could've clawed across the floor to reach them. Some were centuries old, but they didn't look it, each a man of astounding vigor and beauty. Dressed in regal robes and sharp suits, they were dreams on two legs, glowing with riches, and each smiled at his princess.

Except the one who had no princess.

A black goatee stabbed down his chiseled chin. Firm yet delicate hands stuck from the sleeves of a crimson suit. Sapphires shined through his eyes. Sir Hensley DuPont.

The princesses split ways, each to her patron, and then no one stood between Catherine and Sir Hensley. Nostrils flared, he seemed to have caught a scent. He approached with deliberate steps as if the hall had been submerged underwater, until he towered over her. His hand reached toward her, and she imagined it taking hers, kissing the back.

It was happening. She was going to be a princess. Four years of life left, a game of chance meetings, handheld walks, the envy of every common girl in school. Her parents would sign the contract, guaranteeing her family's ascension to high status. At the end, she'd be candied, savored in bits and pieces over time, digested into the great aristocratic bloodline, DuPont. A brief but blessed life.

An outcry of squeals snapped her from the daydream. Hensley's arm stuck past her, his hand gripping another girl's wrist—Emily's. "Pleased to make your acquaintance," he said.

Emily? He'd chosen *Emily?* That gangly bookish nerd?

Bethany appeared at Catherine's side, mouth agape. "I don't believe it."

Catherine couldn't stop trembling. "Why?" she whispered. Emily was plain, a nobody.

But she was one of five siblings. Worse, she had to be delicious. Sir Hensley wouldn't have chosen her otherwise. Her family was always struggling; her parents would sign the contract without delay. She said nothing to her aristocrat, only turned a blank expression to Catherine. Was she gloating?

Catherine couldn't stomach anymore and turned away. It would never be her. It wasn't fair. She ran toward the yellow school buses, the only things that would be picking her up through high school.

Her stomach didn't recover by dinner. She sat at the small round table jammed into her family's cramped kitchen and sulked over a plate of chicken and macaroni casserole while her brother chewed wetly beside her.

Dad and Papa glanced at each other. "Not hungry?" Dad asked.

"If I was a princess, we'd be eating filet mignon," Catherine said.

Dad chuckled. "Don't be in such a rush to grow up. If you were a princess, we'd only have you four more years."

Catherine's fork screeched across her plate. "They'd be perfect years."

"You know, you'll always be our princess," Papa said. "We'd rather have you around years and years."

"Rather than take some monster's blood dowry," Dad added. "If one of them chose you, we wouldn't even sign the contract."

Papa slapped his arm.

Catherine scooted from the table. "Can I be excused?"

She showered upstairs, lathering in two shampoos and drowning her skin in four kinds of scented body wash. "Be delicious," she chanted from shower to bedroom. "Become delicious."

Her dads didn't get it. Neither had ever dreamed of becoming a princess. They foresaw her life as not short and glorious, but long—so, so long. What was so great about that? She'd never be more than middle class at best, watching girls from school vanish as they came of age while she shriveled into her twenties, thirties, endless decaying years.

Her window rattled and she glanced through the glass pane.

Emily hunched outside, her knuckles tapping. A silk dress wrapped her body and jewelry sparkled down her neck and arms in every precious metal known to man and aristocrat. Had she come to gloat again? No, she wouldn't come creeping through the window to do that. Catherine let her in.

Emily slid to the floor and dug her socked feet under scattered laundry. "Hide me."

Catherine eyed her fine clothes. "Why?"

"Are you brainless? I don't want to be a princess."

She couldn't be hearing this. "Yes, you do. Your family lives in a junk heap."

"I don't need an aristocrat's help. I'm already taking college courses. I'll be studying medicine by sixteen." Emily hung her head, examining a dazzling necklace that probably cost more than her parents' car. "I have a plan to get my family on their feet. There's no part in that for some aristocrat turning me into hard candy."

"Hensley likes chocolate." Catherine scoffed. "You're such a nerd. You don't have to study anymore, or even come to school. You're a princess now. Princesses can do whatever they want."

"I want to live!"

Beneath them, the front door banged open. Muffled angry voices climbed through the floor. Catherine couldn't discern the words, but she recognized the voice that didn't belong to her dads—Sir Hensley was in her house.

Emily grabbed Catherine's arm and turned up saucer eyes. She looked like a sparkly slaughterhouse cow. "Hide me!"

Catherine's fingers plucked at the chain that dangled from Emily's neck. A vibrant white-blue diamond watched from its medallion. It was almost funny, looking at them both. So miserable. If only they could swap clothes, jewelry, and take each other's places.

But they couldn't. Beneath her plain face and pretty decorations, Emily was delicious. Catherine was not. Some girls just didn't know how good they had it.

Her gut untwisted as she stared. Poor Emily had despaired for so long that she couldn't see happiness right in front of her. Trapped in low expectations, she feared a better life. What a hell that had to be.

In her moment of weakness, she'd come to a friend for encouragement, and what did Catherine do? Wallow in self-pity. Fixate on envy. She didn't deserve to be a princess.

"I'm sorry," she said, rubbing Emily's grasping claw. "I've been a bad friend. This wonderful thing happened to you and I should be more supportive. You'll get used to it, and then you'll be as full of light as the other princesses. Like you deserve."

Emily recoiled. "That's not—"

Catherine leaned close and smelled Emily's hair. Yes, she was sweet. How had that gone unnoticed all these years? "I'm happy for you. Really." Catherine turned away and opened her mouth wide. "Sir Hensley, she's up here!"

Footsteps charged upstairs and the bedroom door burst open. Sir Hensley stood radiant as ever against humble surroundings. Cold eyes looked past Catherine. He was everything she'd dreamed, and he was where she never thought she'd see an aristocrat—her bedroom.

But not for her.

"There you are," Hensley said, his accent smooth as beckoning fingers. He reached across the room, hand filling Catherine's mind again with visions of being taken, that he'd chosen Emily by mistake, but they were only dreams. She let them slide away as he seized Emily's arm. "Come along. We've a contract."

"But I don't want to!" She held tighter to Catherine's arm, nails pinching. "No, please!"

It was past time to be a good friend. Smiling, Catherine unlatched the fingers that dug into her flesh and locked her reverent eyes with Emily's as Sir Hensley dragged his princess away. "You're *so* lucky."

Elf-Bride

No easy task to marry an elf. They come from the land of Faerie, what used to be part of our world, cut off for centuries. Even mushroom rings won't bridge the way anymore. It takes something blooming wild to take the fair folk's eyes.

But I'm nothing if not wild.

Found a book at this old shop, handwritten before there was hills this side of Scotland. It told how I could summon an elf to wed, and this here lass was old enough to marry.

Mum wouldn't care for it, so I didn't tell her why I was crushing daisies with a hog's bone and old bowl, mixing in honey to slather upon my legs. We humans aren't naturally alluring to the fair folk. Daisy and honey? Feminine essentials.

Weeks later, I brought my best girls to the woods behind the house, where by night we listened to those been lost and died there. They taught us the Fey-Song. At morning, we sang it while we cut the heads off our old dollies with a kitchen knife and set them in the old oak tree. After, I carried the knife out behind the oak and planted the blade between roots for later.

"Aileen, what's the matter with you?" Mum shouted when she saw. As if my girls weren't doing the same.

I couldn't say, *It's obviously a symbolic rite of violence, Mum.* So, I said, "I'm grown. No need for dollies. You knew I'd be a woman someday."

Hurt her, aye, but it was pain she'd need get used to. Wouldn't get easier from there.

A month later, I gathered my girls to the woods again, where we put our backs to the trees and let wild spirits into our heads. It was them that killed the dead of the woods, and they'd curse us if we looked at them.

Daft Melinda. She looked, and from then on she was dead to us. Missed her, we did, but mine wasn't an old book you disobeyed. We cast her out. The rest were bound loyal to my purpose.

After that came the dreams, where spirits taught me courtship dances through flowery fields. Mum said I was having nightmares, kicking the walls and screaming in my sleep, but she weren't in my head.

Silly me, I shrugged at her and said I'd been possessed.

"Be needing a holy man?" she asked.

I almost panicked, but she was only joking. "Nah, Mum. Invited my spirits."

I'd invited other things, too. My old book had warned of their coming. The first night the dreams stopped, I ran into the woods to dance with the men who weren't there. Not dead, not spirits, but something other. Men that never were. Their every whisper laced my thoughts with the never-was, of futures that couldn't be.

Saw Mum's hope for a domesticated daughter. Saw the world retain its green. There was a red-haired woman, unfamiliar, but her toothy smile said I would've loved her my whole life.

Never was. Never to be. I'd come too far for running after such things. Elf eyes watched me. Nothing traveled from Faerie yet, but I had that world's attention and aimed to show my resolve, not let the men who weren't there trap me in the woods. No elf would want a weak bride. Mum's shouting, "Aileen!" led me out from the trees. She'd been awful worried, and I promised peace. The book instructed I be patient until the right time.

Enough patience made me doubt my mettle. What was wrong with me? I was doing unnatural things that couldn't be undone. Didn't like them but couldn't stand to do nothing. The men who weren't there had made that plain as pages and ink.

The old book told of more than elfin courtship. It told of kingdoms, wars, and hatred that hadn't come until long after it was written. Horrors familiar to the fair folk, reasons they exiled themselves to Faerie.

But few prophetic pages remained, and they told me the world was about to get nasty in a big way. Heat of kin to bursting stars. Storms to make dragons look like wasps that would turn our green world gray. Best follow the fair folk's lead and pop off to Faerie. Couldn't say what I'd do there, but that'd be my elf's trouble.

I couldn't stay. Had to see this through to its bloody end.

Eve of the spring equinox, I called my girls over, promised it was time. They dressed pretty, bridesmaids with flowers in their hair.

They began the Fey-Song as they knelt at the old oak, where I pulled my knife from its roots. Grown strong off the land, it had flourished into a brilliant sword. My loyal bridesmaids craned their necks and kept singing the Fey-Song even as I reenacted that day with the dollies. Margaret, Shana, Bonnie—I'd never again feel love like theirs.

Mum ran hollering from the house just as I nestled the last singing bridesmaid into the oak's limbs. She might've interrupted had Faerie's opening not stopped her first.

A midnight sun climbed from the woods and lit a path between the trees. Upon it walked my splendid elf. Tall, dainty, her ears slender, hair mossy, and antlers sharp, she was a dream come true, sunshine in the shape of a woman. She asked my name. I gave it, and I was hers.

I belonged to Faerie.

As we headed off, I looked back and waved goodbye to my bridesmaids, who'd keep singing until the path vanished. Haven't an idea what became of Mum after. Never looked back again, either. In Faerie, every taste, smell, and touch is so intense that time and thought drift into fog.

That keeps me distracted from the dread that awaits my old world. No point gazing into future fires that'll shrivel even the memory of home and friends. No use wondering on the hurt coming for Mum, and spirits, and that red-haired woman I'll never meet but whose smile I would've loved forever. Best throw myself into every wild frolic at my elf-bride's side, caring not for what's left behind.

And I'm nothing if not wild.

Aggressive Mimicry

Miguel told himself it wasn't love anymore. Love was a dream he had buried months ago when he saw Omar and Jessica behind the mall, Omar's hand up her shirt. There had been a rough patch then, but they stayed friends. Miguel could live with being friends. He had lived with worse.

But then sometimes Omar would touch him.

Not that he blushed every time. There was friendly jostling, shoving, slapping on the back, and Miguel would've gone crazy if every little thing set him off. But there were other times. That bus ride from Detroit that Miguel had to tease him about later for appearances, when Omar fell asleep and his head shifted to Miguel's shoulder. That day Omar leaned over Miguel's lap to grab a twenty he spotted wedged under a bench. Or that one afternoon—

There were dozens of memories. Small, nothing anyone else would bother holding onto, but Miguel replayed them a hundred times. He had buried the dream of love, but at those times he might visit the grave and pray.

This time, Omar put his arm around Miguel's neck, nothing serious, but then pulled him close to tell a secret. The stupid underbelly of Miguel's thoughts couldn't help wondering if it meant something deeper.

It never would. A hundred yards away, Jessica's friends were fawning over the sight of Omar—his curly black locks, his two-day stubble; an action movie star in the flesh. They didn't care he had no money, no job, no prospects now that high school was past. He would sneak one of them into the movies tonight, something new like *Back to the Future* or *Mad Max: Beyond Thunderdome*, and spend half the runtime locking tongues.

Not Miguel. There were days he felt so touch-starved that he could understand why people like him broke down, married a girl, let their parents sigh in relief, and embraced the misery of peace. No one suspected, far as he knew. He was always out with Omar, and Omar was straight as they come; all the girls orbited him. Surely Miguel would pick up his scraps. So people let him be. He and Omar remained friends.

"I couldn't hear you," Miguel said when the whispering ended.

"You want me to stick my tongue in your ear?" Omar pulled Miguel closer and made to bite at his earlobe.

"No, I want you to shout it, loud as you can, you butt."

Omar pressed his forehead into Miguel's hair and whispered again. "Roman's brother told him there's a woman who's been swimming in the pond every night this past week. We're going to see her."

"Think she's the weeping ghost?"

Omar recoiled with a scowl. "Don't be a numbskull. You're here thinking about little kid ghost stories while she's out there swimming naked in the moonlight."

"How'd she get up there?" Miguel raised an arm against Omar's slap and laughed. "See? I am a numbskull." And he was going. Not that he cared about a naked woman, but Omar was going so of course Miguel was going.

Even with Roman going, which meant David was going, and David was a punk.

They gathered at dusk on the sandy side of the pond. The shore was desolate, only crushed soda cans and paper cups to tell people sometimes visited. Rainfall had been worse than usual the past week. What was most often an overblown puddle now spread as wide as a lake, if nowhere as deep, and had attracted uncommon fauna to the shore. Various birds and water bugs danced around each other, each trying to catch its next meal. Miguel paused to watch a small brown bird hidden among the rocks lure bugs to its tongue by pretending it was a worm and slurp them into its beak when they fell for it.

The young men piled the few dry sticks they could find and built a fire on the sand to ward off birds and bugs alike.

"Can we still see her with the firelight?" David asked. He was skinny and the youngest of six siblings. Gaunt shadows danced beneath his face. "Maybe she won't come."

"Israel said they had their headlights on just to mess with her and she didn't care," Roman said. He was all smiles. "But they were on the road, so maybe she didn't think anything of it."

Omar kicked at the fire. Embers flew toward the darkening sky. "But she's hot, right?"

"Hot as fire. Gorgeous face, body to kill for, and in the moonlight you could see it all."

Omar whistled, impressed.

Miguel imagined they had seen naked women in magazines before and couldn't guess what made the prospect of this one so tantalizing. Maybe because she was a mystery. More likely because what she was doing was none of their business.

"What will you say to her, Romeo?" he asked.

Roman opened his mouth, but Omar raised his hand to stop him. "He didn't ask *Roman*, he asked *Romeo*. What will I say? I'll say, 'Miss, can you do us a favor? Our friend Miguel's more a virgin than Mary herself, so if you'd help him with that we'd appreciate it. He doesn't want to give birth this Christmas.'"

Roman laughed because he thought it was funny. Miguel laughed because he was supposed to, and wondered if there might come a day when men could have children with other men. It seemed too much to hope. Maybe in the movies.

David didn't laugh. He stood up. "Don't blaspheme."

Omar got in his face. "Did you hear me blaspheme? I didn't take the Lord's name in vain or nothing." He grinned. "For Christ's sake."

That set David off, and he tackled Omar. They scuffled in the sand as Roman kept laughing. Miguel only watched. Omar could win easy, but he would let David pin him for the sake of peace. If there was a woman who swam here, she would pluck Omar out of the group for sure and Miguel wouldn't blame her. He would replay his memories.

Roman clapped his shoulder. "You're looking pretty intense, friend. You want to join in, back up your girlfriend?"

Omar was already down by then, half his face in the sand. He gave in, and David relented. They stood, grinned, and dusted themselves off.

"Sun's about set, moon's bright." Omar's finger traced the sky from the sand to the crescent moon as if making a measurement. "Think I'll take a leak before the main event."

Roman said he'd go, too, so together they climbed up the sand toward the road.

Miguel stared at the moon's expressionless mouth. The dream was not dead. He remembered the night when he wrote a love letter about Omar's hand reaching up Jessica's shirt and how it might as well have been Miguel's chest, to rip his heart out. Later he burned the letter and buried the ashes behind his house. No one could have a chance to read it.

Buried, but not dead.

Watching Omar fight in the firelight, listening to him joke, Miguel still wanted Omar's love. He wanted to feel Omar's desire the way Jessica did. The way tonight's woman might if she was even real.

David's gruff voice pulled Miguel from the moon. "Didn't go with them?"

"Didn't have to go."

"I know. But you're passing up a chance to see Omar with his jeans open. Roman didn't pass it up."

Miguel froze.

Did he——? No. David didn't know his feelings. He didn't know anything.

"You passed it up, too. What the hell's wrong with us?"

Miguel laughed.

David glared across the fire. "One of these days, somebody with a camera's going to see you seeing him, and then he'll see you seeing him. Then it's over for you."

"If you say so," Miguel muttered, but realized a moment too late that nothing he said could convince David to leave it alone. He'd only minutes ago scuffled with Omar but was ready to throw down again. That was all he wanted. If Miguel had been riled enough he would've stood and gotten in David's face. To say it with words alone wouldn't do.

Omar and Roman came to the rescue. "Wake up, lads," Omar said. "There she is."

They jogged down the sandy slope and helped David and Miguel kick the fire out. The smoking wood remained aglow, but under the brilliance of the moon that was nothing.

And it really was brilliant, Miguel thought. He'd never seen a crescent moon light the surface of the water as bright as a full moon this way.

It lit the woman in the water. No one had seen her enter, but there she swam in the pond, her arms cresting the surface with each stroke. From this far, Miguel couldn't see her all that well. He wasn't sure how Roman's brother had determined her beauty.

Omar jabbed an elbow into Miguel's side. "Not scared, right? Doesn't look like a ghost."

Miguel imagined not, but under the harsh moonlight, she might've been anything.

"I know what to say." Omar winked and then cupped his hands around his mouth. "Hey, sweetheart! Not bad swimming out there! You want, I can teach you the breaststroke!" David and Roman laughed.

She stopped swimming. Her arms settled into a float, and then she stood. Miguel couldn't remember the depth of the pond, the drought crater had always lain uneven, but he didn't think anyone could stand that tall at its center.

But the thought flaked apart, a clump of wet sand tossed into the water. The still-brightening moon said there was only beauty here, beauty everlasting. Even at this distance her luminescence was inescapable. If the moonlight was milk across the shape of her then it had come from some heavenly cow milked by God himself. Every inch promised to boil the blood, every magnificent finger ensured a lightning bolt of splendor.

Miguel only saw her with his eyes, but the others stood transfixed, their blood a deluge of raging hormones and desires in every place that made them weak. A pulse rocketed through the air, high-pitched like an alarm. Each beat tugged the young men toward the water.

David was first to break. He didn't speak, only panted as he tore his shoes off and darted through sand and water. Blood seeped from his ears. His jeans fell away, and he was still fighting with his shirt as his middle sank below the surface. Roman had a little more trouble tearing off his shoes, but then he took off on David's heels.

Omar was right behind him.

Somehow, as he splashed knee-deep into the pond, the spell of the moonlit woman waned enough for him to pause and glance back to shore. "Miguel?"

Miguel hadn't moved an inch. He was the only one still fully-clothed. "I don't think I can." He looked from Omar to the moonlit lady, the seductress of the pond. Her arms hung at her sides, her expressionless face carved from exquisite marble. "I can't."

"You can." Omar beamed. "You can do this. We can all do this. She's right there and she wants us. Don't you feel it?"

"I feel—" Miguel looked back to Omar. He couldn't fault the three of them—their blood pounding, the light pulling, the air ringing, everything inside telling them to go for it—when everything inside him said the same. "I feel love."

Omar nodded. "I think I love her, too."

"For you. I ... love you." Miguel's throat narrowed. "I only wanted you."

Omar went on beaming through his rugged stubble, his eager eyes reflecting the radiant moon. "Christ, Miguel, I know that."

Miguel's heart hammered his rib cage. "Since when?"

"Since you saw me with Jessica. I've had my heart broken before. I knew the look on your face."

If Omar knew the look and the feeling, he had to know that pitiful, microscopic spark of hope that lived in every aching heart, the one that thought just maybe the person of affection would love him back against all odds. The dream, resurrected from its grave by a crescent moon.

"And?" Miguel asked.

"And? What do you think we came out here for? I'm trying to help you."

"I don't want her help. I want you."

Omar's body shuddered like a heartbeat, every blood vessel aching to go. He tore his gaze from Miguel and charged deeper into the water. It was a miracle he'd resisted this long. The air's pulse hit a heart attack panic so insistent that blood ran from Omar's eyes.

"Don't," Miguel whispered as his knees trembled.

David and Roman had almost reached the moonlit woman, but Omar was catching up. The only time Miguel saw him nude and it was while he ran to someone else. Miguel took off his shoes. They had come out here together, hadn't they? As it had always been; Omar was going, so Miguel was going, too. He didn't know what any of them would do when they got there, but he was going.

He made it ankle-deep into the water before he looked again to the moonlit woman. She raised her arms wide to each side, welcoming her suitors to visit her, to come drink the milky light that ran down her breasts. *Drink deep, drink it all in,* her body seemed to say.

Miguel managed to stop as the boiling heat of his blood eased across his body. Closer now, the effect she had on the others ran sideways in him, sliding away from her. Now he saw her as being less coated in luxurious moonlight and more shrouded within it, a mask gifted to her by the crescent arc in the sky. The beauty that drove Omar's lust was an illusion.

Miguel flinched back. "Omar, wait!"

Omar had nearly reached her. He and the others were only bobbing heads and arms, but the water climbed no higher than her thighs, where between them her nethers still shone white, even as the illusion faded.

"Come back! It's not real!"

Omar beckoned Miguel with an enthusiastic wave. Then he and Roman and David somehow arrived at the woman's waist together, their heads beneath her hips. She sank upon them, arms closing in, the curtain of hungry moonlight across her face impenetrable to Omar, but to Miguel it was only a lunar veil. Through that veil, even at this distance, he made out luminous teeth.

"It's not real!" Miguel shouted again. He stumbled and fell into the gentle, lapping waves thrown his way by the charging young men. "I'm real. I'm here and I'm real!"

The light burned brighter, blinding Miguel, its ringing pulse deafening, about to snap, and then the crescent moon dimmed. Every wave stilled. The pond grew too dark to make out its center. If the woman and her suitors were still out there, Miguel couldn't see them and he didn't hear a thing.

His thoughts became abstract, less sentences and more impulses. He dove into the blackened waters and shouted for Omar, choking out gulping mouthfuls of the pond at each stroke, but there was no answer. No moonlit woman came for him.

Rising from the surface, he grasped at the space where Omar's head last crested and came away with nothing. "I would've followed you anywhere, even with Jessica, with anyone. But you had to have this—well, fine then! I'm going to meet someone else, you hear me? I'm leaving, and I'm going to be happy the rest of my life. But there's no rest of our lives for you, because you fucking threw it away!"

Miguel thrashed at the pond, and a shudder ran up his gut, out his mouth, and into the water. He paddled back to shore, where he fell on the sand, spent. His gaze did not leave the pond except to glance at the sky, where the faint crescent moon smiled out of reach. Grass stirred with buzzing mosquitos. A brown bird that'd played its tongue for a worm now nestled between two rocks, its belly filled.

Where the young men once sat, Miguel stirred the glowing fire back to life. If Omar was out there, he might see it and drag himself to shore.

He wouldn't. Miguel knew that. The moon made no light of its own, reflecting only what it stole. But just in case, Miguel waited. The grave of the dream needed tending and perhaps, when summer dried the canal, so would other graves.

Seven Signs He Doesn't Love You

Donnie comes home with puppy eyes and Korean takeout. "We're going to Keso."

You've only arrived five minutes before him, still wearing scrubs from the hospital. The island name is familiar. Some place in the Mediterranean or the Philippines, you can't recall.

"Two weeks," he goes on. "Fun in the sun, not a care in the world."

It's not the vacation you had in mind. You say nothing, but your disappointment is loud.

His face slackens. He hears the emptiness where your gleeful squealing should bounce off the walls. "Did I mess up?"

You smile, but your reassurance is only at half-mast. "No, it'll be fun."

Sign 1: He Didn't Even Ask

You don't want to be difficult. You're not that kind of girlfriend. Sometimes you can't help it, and he puts up with the shift switches, late nights, early morning alarms. But this is a vacation, and he's already booked the tickets. Make the best of it.

The island of Keso might be fun in the sun in a nicer season, but you aren't visiting then. You're here now. The wind is playful, tossing your hair into your face, but already it's whining through the trees on the far edge of a temper tantrum. Not long from now it will rise into a screaming fit and pull your hair, and only the next change of seasons will calm it.

You're here in the off-season because it's cheaper, but Donnie doesn't put it that way. "It'll be more laidback." He flashes reassuring teeth.

A mustached man in white shirt and khakis leans into the boat while a pretty, smiling woman with hip-length hair greets Donnie. White sands bask over much of the island, dotted with green plants you don't know and towering palm trees, barren of fruit.

Enough pale clouds drift to cast sunrays and keep the sand from getting too hot. You could lie on this beach half-naked, let the fleeting sunshine stroke your skin while you listen to white and green waves lick the coastline. This might not be so bad. You'll have to remind Donnie to lather sunblock or he'll be red as the sloping shingled rooftops of the buildings here. He never remembers on his own.

The mustached man pulls your bags from the boat. The wheels go *thunk-thunk* over each plank of aged wooden dock. Sores pockmark its beams where barnacles have grown in the past, perhaps beneath rising tides. There's a beauty in the anticipated tempest and a promise that the island has survived this before and will survive it again. You're comforted as you follow the mustached man, the smiling, chattering woman, and your strutting boyfriend.

You're less comforted when you approach check-in. What you see plants a scream in your throat, but you choke on it before you embarrass yourself.

Donnie is asking the smiling woman about activities that the weather will likely preclude. The things that frighten you at the visitor center are only scenery to him. You, too, might be scenery for all he acknowledges your dismay before he hears what isn't there—your expected murmured agreement.

Sign 2: He Doesn't Notice These Ghastly Grins

You point. His eyes follow your gaze to hunched stone characters, each knee-high, fashioned in the shapes of monkeys, lions, and dragons. Each bares an oversized grin beneath round, wild eyes. Chiseled whiskers, brows, and manes flow against stone faces, down stone necks. Their hands and claws are flecked with green residue, long battered by the sea and storms, yet still standing.

Donnie guffaws. "Like a Halloween funhouse. You scared?"

The smiling woman approaches, her bare feet almost touching your white tennis shoes. She is a few inches shorter than you, but her voluminous hair makes her seem so much grander. "These are Raggi," she says. "Island guardian spirits. They watch over Keso so that everyone has a good time. They love to see you here. They're happy."

That you do not doubt, but joy in the eyes isn't joy in the teeth. The gleeful stares are discordant with the angry teeth, as if pieces of separate creatures.

Donnie smiles. "See? Nothing to be scared of."

You're not scared. Disturbed.

"I thought you liked these things."

He's referring to your collection. In the apartment, you have a curio where you keep small statuettes and figurines. There is no theme; they aren't a particular animal, or from a specific mythology, culture, or media franchise. Their only common element is that you're fond of them. Your collection is nothing like these grinning creatures.

Donnie rolls his eyes. "Didn't you hear Lala? Guardian spirits. It's normal here. Don't be xenophobic."

"Who's Lala?" you ask.

He nods to the pretty smiling woman. She turns her beaming teeth at you, friendlier than the statues or at least she wants you to think so, but the effect is lost. You're already rattled. She doesn't share your apprehension for these ghastly grins. Neither does the rest of the staff.

"They're giving me a headache," you say. It gets better when you close your eyes, let the sun massage your skin, and breathe the sea's salty scents.

"Keso is cleansing," Lala says. "Relax, and you don't need to think anymore. Then, no more headache."

"I'll try that."

Men and women stroll past with luggage and duffel bags on their backs. They load the same boat you arrived on. They'll be heading home with the season wrapping up, only minimal staff remaining to attend minimal guests. The resort will become a ghost town.

Donnie finishes the lingering paperwork at the check-in desk and then the mustached man takes you and your bags along wooden walkways to a small house that overlooks the western beach. Each house is a duplex, but it's the off-season. No one lives on the other side.

Once you're settled, Donnie suggests you head to the bazaar before it closes. That sounds like a fun, vacation-y thing to do. You change into shorts and breathable blouse, a straw hat on your head and shades on your eyes.

You almost forget the statues until you head outside and notice them nestled to either side of your door, a brazen dragon and a monkey who peers through green ferns. You're not sure how you didn't notice them when you came in. Other statues decorate the beach, where they face the ocean. They aren't settled close to the water, but you can't lie on the sand without falling under their gaze.

Donnie notices your hesitation and rolls his eyes again. "For real? Just ignore them. You'll want a souvenir."

A small grinning lion for your curio, perhaps? You think not, but you let Donnie lead you. No sense spending your vacation hidden indoors with your nose in a book. You can do that anywhere. It would be nice if he didn't roll his eyes, but in some ways you're used to that.

You spot a dark-haired shape down the walkway. Lala's smile breaks open, her hands clasped beneath her chest. "Finally, she emerges! We're so happy." You're not sure who "we" refers to, and you don't want to know. She's starting to remind you of the ditzy girls you were friends with in high school, years you'd rather forget. Donnie trails behind her and you behind him, all the way to the bazaar at the island's center.

You try to ignore the statues on your way. They're common as trees.

Keso's bazaar is two rows of wooden stalls to either side of an open plaza, the sand covered in thin, colorful blankets, the stands hidden beneath crimson and violet canopies. They're manned by bald, sunbaked men who sell fruit and pretty, sun-kissed women who sell jewelry. Their small daughters lace seashells onto necklaces. White placards with black letters tell you where you might have signed up for waterskiing and scuba diving, but the off-season has chased those activities away. No one will take boats out for pleasure when the storms come.

The Raggi statues watch the bazaar as if guarding against thieves. You angle your shades so that the stem covers your peripheral vision. The fewer grins you see, the better.

One stall catches your attention, its wood warped by seawater at its base. A skeletal elderly woman sits in a patchwork cushiony seat behind and fans herself with a strip of white cardboard. She chomps at a cigar and blue smoke dances between her lips. She reminds you of the Caterpillar from *Alice in Wonderland*, but she does not ask who you are just yet.

"What's your pleasure, miss?" she asks with a smoker's charred tone.

You aren't sure. The woman's stall bears a treasure trove of small stone figures, some gray-skinned, others onyx or pearlescent. They're simple figures, none so detailed as Keso's grinning guardians, but you like them better. Their minimalist shapes convey meaning through body language.

You've seen the ouroboros before. Here is a human equivalent to the snake eating its own tail, a man whose legs are bent backward, shoved into his mouth, eager to devour his thighs, his lower spine, everything. There's something vulgar about him, but also tantalizing.

"You like him?" the smoking woman asks. "He might like you." She cackles out a mouthful of smoke.

You smile, liking her instantly, and become careless. "I'd like the island better if the statues everywhere looked like yours, ma'am." The cackle deflates into a cough, and you realize you've offended her. Hands raised, pleading, you apologize. "The Raggi are your heritage. I should be more respectful."

"I'm more offended by ma'am. It makes me sound old." Her skeleton hand reaches over the stall. She introduces herself as Milan, and you introduce yourself in return.

Before you can explain the etymology of your name, Milan points her cigar at a monkey statue across the plaza. His grin is too detailed even fifty feet away.

"The statues aren't the Raggi," she explains. "The Raggi have no bodies, being spirits. They travel the world on black storm clouds, coming and going from Keso. The statues are vessels for when they return here, not so different from you tourists and the houses we set for you. Keso is an island always waiting to be filled. Stormy season is haunting season."

You wonder what Lala of "Keso is cleansing" fame would say to that, but to Milan you only stammer out an apology for your foreign faux pas.

"Storms get worse every year, longer haunting season. Someday, storms will live here, lightning Keso's only tourist." Milan waves her hand, wiping a smoky snake from the air. "No offense. Better to know the dangers now, while the statues are empty, and even then you can do everything right yet still displease the spirits. The Raggi are not guardians. Only travelers. You're a traveler, been with travelers. You know how irate they can be."

You look across the plaza, not to the statues, but to Donnie. He stands beside a produce stall, where Lala and a wrinkled man show him how to cut a durian. He's acclimated so easily to Keso that you should ask if he's visited before.

"But some travel for love," Milan says. "Is that you? Do you hope to find love on Keso the way that man has found our Lala?"

You titter, hand over your mouth. "That's Donnie. My boyfriend."

Milan stiffens. "Did you visit Keso to lose him?" she asks, which makes you laugh harder.

You explain, best you can, that Donnie has always been a people person, the kind who touches shoulders, clasps hands, leans in when listening. Even now, he's brushing a stray curly lock out of Lala's eyes. You notice every gesture, every give and flow of body language, same as you notice every Raggi statue, but unlike those stone animals you see nothing sinister behind Donnie's behavior. He's said before, you can't put two and two together, but you can see the number four hidden in a haystack.

"I've been ornery," you say. "He might just want someone else to talk to."

Milan scoffs. "He might want to roll his tongue back into his mouth."

You're not sure if she's serious. You aren't jealous; you're not that kind of girlfriend. "He loves me," you say. "I'm not worried. We have fun together."

"Oh yes, a boyfriend is fun. But you can't let him drag you behind forever. Someday, you'll need a man."

"What, like a doctor?"

"No one said anything about jobs. But a man, however he's born, whatever he does, has attentiveness and responsibility. That's what you'll need, and your boy there isn't it. Here, you should have this." She places the ouroboros in your palm.

You try to pay, but she won't accept.

"No one buys on the line between seasons. I will be going soon. You're sweet. A little funny, but so am I." Milan waves her cigar again. "Take it and remember me. And sort out your heart."

You promise that you will. Donnie is waving, suggesting he's done, time to go. You start to leave Milan's stall, but there's an urge you can only fight for so long.

Your eyes glance over your shoulder. "Smoking will kill you, you know."

Milan inhales and the cigar's end glows in her eyes. "It will try."

At day's end, you and Donnie watch the ship leave with most of the staff, other tourists, and merchants. You think you see Milan, but there are too many people trying to leave. It's almost a warning.

Donnie places his hands on your shoulders. "It'll be like we have the island to ourselves."

You suppose you'll feel that way when it's just the two of you indoors, with no Lala and no statues. You follow Donnie to one of the outdoor diners and then back to the house where you're staying. Maybe you feel nothing off his touching Lala, but your eyes notice the strand of her hair that clings to his sweat-dotted shoulder, the graze of lipstick on his arm. The Raggi monkey behind his brush watches you enter the house and close the door.

Donnie pulls you near, expectant, but you shrink away. "What?" he asks. "The statues again?"

You don't answer. Yes, but no. It's many things.

"You're crazy. That's okay. Crazy girls are always best in bed." Right, the important part. How could you focus on anything else? "Come on. You have no sense of humor sometimes, you know that?"

"Maybe you're not funny." It blurts from between your lips, seeping like Milan's smoke.

"What the hell is the problem? Come on, just tell me."

You try, but you already know his excuses.

Sign 3: He Says It's Your Imagination

By the time he's done ranting, he's in tears and you feel like shit.

"It hurts that you'd ever think of me that way, you know that?" he says. "My ex, I don't know if you remember."

You do, but you won't speak up.

"She wouldn't even let me be friends with girls. She was crazy, I mean real deal crazy. You're not like that." He grabs his bag with his cash inside. "I'm heading to the bar. One of us has to have a good time on this vacation." He hesitates, likely to see if you'll stop him, and you're paralyzed over whether you should. When you do nothing, he storms out the door, where dusk has painted the sky a dark orange.

You meant to say that you didn't want to be alone. The edge of the monkey statue pokes outside the open door. You slam it shut against the whining wind and sink onto the bed, your only company the statuette that Milan has gifted you.

You're ruining this vacation. He took the trouble of making all travel arrangements, yet here you are glaring daggers at an innocent woman who's only doing her job. Except, do you really feel it's your fault? Aren't you entitled to the benefit of a doubt? You could let the whole Lala thing go if he would show one spoonful of concern for how the Raggi statues bother you. Tender arms closed around yours, fingers stroking your hair, soft lips in your ear that tell you it's okay you feel this way, you're loved, you're safe, you're not a burden.

You hear and feel none of these things when you shut off the lights. There's only darkness, wind, and surf for the longest time, and then a noise outside. Not Donnie. No, it's farther away at first.

You hear someone rise from the crashing tide. That's not a sound you could possibly distinguish from the waves, and there's breaking water, the soft plop of feet on waterlogged sand, the pattering seawater dripping across the dry beach and toward the houses.

You wake when the wind snaps the door out of Donnie's hand, slamming it behind him. The house is dark, its only noise the subtle rattle of windowpanes as the wind seeks another way in. He had been trying to come quiet so not to disturb you.

How late is it? You flip the light on. "You were gone a long while."

He smiles. There's drink in his eyes. "Oh, I met Lala at the bar."

Of course.

He notices the look on your face. "Listen, you would really like her. She's funny, smart but not the same way you are." He lies across the bed, stinking with sweat but making no movements toward stripping and showering. "I think you'd get on pretty good."

There's an unspoken conversation here, another partner in the house with you. He knows about your exes, of all kinds. Maybe you can't put two and two together, but it isn't like you've never seen a math problem before. He isn't hiding her the way a man hides a mistress.

No, he wants you to befriend her. You know what he wants, the same thing too many have approached you two about. *Why not make it three?* they ask. And telling them you don't want to, well, that never seems enough for them.

You change the subject. "How many Raggi statues do you think are on this island?"

The bed ripples under his exaggerated shrug.

You wonder aloud whether the kinds of statues come in even numbers, whether there's a chimeric statue that merges monkey, lion, and dragon into one creature with three evil grins. How many years have they been here? How many years of storms will it take to erode them to featureless rocks?

You think that's how you'd like Keso. Take the sea like it's a strip of sandpaper and rub out the edges of its personality until it doesn't bother you anymore. That's how incompatible you are with Keso. It isn't like you don't appreciate Donnie having booked the trip, but you and Keso don't mix. There are other inexpensive places. Places without the statues. You just can't be around them. You feel them creeping, watching for weakness.

"Can you understand?" you ask. Having voiced your fear, you wait to feel his arms around yours, his lips in your ear that tell you it's okay you feel this way, you're loved, you're safe, you're not a burden.

His sudden snore jerks your attention over your shoulder.

Sign 4: He Cannot Listen

In the days since, you drift along the beach, hardly seeing him. As it turns out, you can't stay at the house for long, either. Every moment you try to distract yourself with music, a book, Milan's statuette, you feel prying eyes, as if the monkey and the dragon statues are peering in your windows. You've tried lugging them down the walkway but they're immovable, as if carved from a larger rock upon which the house sits.

Even on the beach the statues watch, nestled in green growth. You near the water, sometimes wading into the tide, but their gaze is inescapable.

Only Donnie is escapable. You've made excuses not to see him, eat with him, and at night you don't touch each other. Some nights he isn't there at all. If he's laughing with Lala, well, you don't think about that. In another few days this vacation will end and your life will return to normal. Whatever weakness has wormed its way into your muscles and bones, it will leave.

You don't blame him or yourself. You blame the statues.

At the horizon, the wind tugs at black clouds, riling them up. They'll take their anger out not on the wind, but will misdirect it at the innocent, at the island. You see narrow lightning bolts stitch between the bulbous black clouds. It's only a matter of time.

As your eyes drift down from the horizon and focus on the sand, you notice footprints coming from the water. No one else has been here; you've been alone. The tide should have washed them away—*is* washing them away as you stare.

At the house, the wind tugs at windows, desperate fingers prying at the house. It wants in worse than ever.

You wish Donnie would act like you had the island to yourselves, that you were his only company. Despite the vacuous space he pries wide open within you, you still love him. You love his musky scent. You love that he volunteers as a school crossing guard, that he protects people for a living. You even love the things your friends tell you not to, the way he sometimes smacks your backside in passing, the way he holds you down some nights. His blood tosses under hurricane winds, and every gust sweeps you off your feet.

If you didn't love him, you wouldn't have let him take you to Keso.

Just the same, concern hounds you, its feet planted in your footsteps so that you can't see its path when you look back, yet you feel its glare when you face ahead.

No Donnie at the house, and you hardly care. Exhausted from circling the island, you can hardly change before you lie across the bed and hope the ocean lulls you to sleep. Darkness creeps in with the tide.

You hear footsteps from the beach again, breaking water, someone climbing the sand. The footsteps only pause when someone's wet skin rubs against a Raggi statue, a sandpapery scrape. Your ears can't tell what kind, but you guess it wasn't a lion. There's no lion outside your rental house, and the scraping ends just as your door whips open.

It's coming.

It's in the room with you, covering you in a blanket of blackness, and it won't stop shouting. You're tired, can hardly move until the blackness folds around you, the footsteps in your ears.

It's coming.

Arms hold you in the dark, you're loved, you're safe, you're together in the dark, and you scream loud as you please. You don't have to worry about thin apartment walls, about neighbors and the busy street. No biting the insides of your cheek, no holding it in your chest. It's a free, gleeful moment where you're so loud you hurt your own ears.

You're coming.

You snap awake and sit upright. Sweat coats every inch of skin, and there's an earthquake between your legs. The blackness is only night, the shouting only distant thunder. You've never had a dream like that, never woken up feeling shaken, and hurry to the shower where you wash the dream off your skin.

It's not until you emerge that you realize no one else is in the house.

Sign 5: Vacation for Two, So Why Are You Alone?

But you're not alone. Donnie's not here, but something is. You only feel alone in the rare moments you spend with Donnie. You're less alone when he's gone than when he's around.

You circle the island for a sixth day in a row and then head back. You're hardly eating anymore, only a salad here, a banana there. Sleep comes hard. You keep waking from dreams. You almost prefer the dreams to exhausted daylight when you wander the island in a hazy trance.

You said you wanted to rub out the edges of the island's personality, but it seems more like that's what Keso is doing to you. It's a hungry island, suckling at your breast until you're empty, and then what? Another empty vessel.

Donnie isn't home again. This wouldn't surprise you except, with the wind picking up, you thought he might return by dusk. Only the peeping monkey greets you at the door. It grins after you on your way down the wooden walkway.

It isn't alone, of course. There's the dragon. There are the pairs of statues outside every doorway. They line the walkway, some close, some distant, and stare out at the beach, darkening beneath the coming storm. The plaza is empty now, all merchants gone home near a week ago, but the statues remain. Perhaps they have something to sell, if only you'd approach. What's your pleasure, miss?

You start to run, as if the statues can chase, and then you slow to a jog in case they can. Wouldn't want to encourage them.

Lights flicker between windows, the power having a hiccup. If it has to hold its breath and let the darkness seep across Keso, maybe the statues' power will fade. You close your eyes—no, their gaze remains. You run again, but don't cry out. The worst statue might hear you, the mythical dragon-monkey-lion chimera, King of Raggi, King of Keso.

Heart clawing at your lungs, you stop outside a doorway and lean one arm on the wall to catch your breath. Quiet puffs flow in and out.

Never mind being the easy girlfriend. You'll tell him to hold you, tell him the things to say. He can be a good boyfriend for a change. Not nice, not charming. Good. Responsible. Attentive. You wish Milan hadn't left so fast. Maybe she heeded her own warnings, fled ahead of the storm, the Raggi. You should have gone with her.

A sound slips into your ears beneath the howling wind. Familiar, scandalous, you first heard it in your college dorm when the girl next door and her roommate were reunited after spring break. Heavy breathing breaks into a soft, feminine moan.

Deeper, another moan washes the first away. And this second moan is more familiar. Too familiar.

You creep past the twin lions that brace this doorway, along one darkened window, and listen through the glass. Closed curtains block the room and it would be too dark to see anyway. It doesn't change what you hear, a sound you should have heard in your bed here, have heard many nights in your apartment, though back home you'd make him moan harder, louder, embarrass him a little at how good you make him feel. She's not able to do that, but he doesn't seem to mind.

Your heart no longer claws inside your lungs. It doesn't want out, because then it might have to feel without the protection of your ribs, muscles, and skin. A different sort of pain bleeds through its atriums and ventricles.

The lion statues at the door carry on their evil grins. As if they knew. As if it was their goal all along to drive you here and force you to know.

Sign 6: It's Not Your Imagination

You run and don't know where you're headed. Not to the house where he might find you, lie to you, oblivious to what you've seen while he wears her stink across his skin.

Since when? The first night you arrived, after you fell asleep?

Milan tried to warn you, but you couldn't put two and two together.

You're pursued again, not by concern but by the sound of his moaning, beating behind you like footsteps. Him, her, they slide across your skin, carried in the wind, as if you're sandwiched between them in bed, just like he wanted.

Another stranger's unlit house, another break for panting and pain, this time before a window. At last, you see yourself. A reflection?

No, it's you, but through his eyes. He likes having you around the way he likes a video game, something he can pick up, play with, and put down as he pleases. This was never a vacation for two. You came to Keso because he wanted it. Your enjoyment is incidental; your approval and affection are payment he's owed for his magnanimous presence in your life. That you've withheld them shows ingratitude. He finds affection elsewhere even though he's been irresponsible, inattentive, cold.

The horizon is only blackness now, the storm looming overhead. Clouds burst with rain, and you don't mind that it soaks your clothes and skin. He won't be able to come looking for you until the storm is over. More time to be alone, as if you haven't had enough.

You dread keeping this to yourself the rest of the trip, sharing a boat and then plane ride with him until you can divide your life from his. You wish you could share this revelation with Milan, but she's gone.

The beach calls as rain spits bullet holes in the sand. You search for footprints but find nothing. Water sweeps everything away. Wasn't someone looking for you?

When you return to the house, you find shattered white debris on the floor. It's Milan's ouroboros, the man who eats himself, now broken into a dozen pieces. Thunder must have shaken the furniture and made it fall. Why couldn't the Raggi statues shatter instead? Too important? Too expectant of their own guests? Couldn't the guests shatter, too?

It's your fault. You were too difficult a girlfriend, even though you didn't want to be. If only you'd been more open to Keso's cleansing, showed gratitude as it smoothed out the edges of your personality, then maybe he'd still be with you instead of *her.*

Someone approaches. You know it isn't a dream this time—you aren't even in bed. The footsteps should be impossible to hear under wind, rain, and thunder, under the aggressive tide, but they're loud and clear as they climb the sand and approach the house.

Sign 7: He Doesn't Coil Your Soul Across Infinity, Let You Devour Everything You Are. He is Selfish. What Does He Matter? There's Something About You. Why, You Belong Here, Don't You? Yes, We Think So. Stop Fighting. Yes, We Love You. He Doesn't. Let Go. Don't You Want To? Give to Us, No Fight, Give Love, Give, Give.

You're unsure how long you've been asleep, how many days and nights. If there was a dream, you don't remember it. You awaken and everything's a blur, not only your memory, but your feelings, thoughts, all of it. Like you're empty. Donnie sleeps beside you, and you smile at him. What a lovely boyfriend. You're so lucky.

Alone, you step outside past smiling statues and look to the coast. The storm has passed. There will be more before the season ends, but for now, the sky is at peace.

Keso has cleansed.

It's a shame you're leaving today. Maybe next time you'll come during the tourist season, enjoy the activities and nicer weather. Or maybe you'll visit in the haunting season again, while the island awaits storms and spirits. Either way, there will be a next time, because Donnie liked it, and you did, too. You aren't going to be difficult now.

When he awakens, you enjoy one last walk on the beach together. Lala kicks across the sand to say farewell, wish safe travels, and hug you both. You disliked her but can't imagine why. She's just the sweetest, and you'll miss her.

After your walk, you and Donnie pack. A man takes your bags to the dock, wheels once more going *thunk-thunk* over wooden planks, and each strike feels like a step over your grave. You aren't sure why.

"Doing okay?" Donnie asks, in a way where there's only one right answer.

"Absolutely," you say, smiling. You kiss his cheek and start toward the boat. You'll watch the island shrink until it vanishes and imagine it's been wiped from the world until it sees you again. It almost resembles a stranger now that the wind has relaxed.

You can't help feeling, as you board the boat, that you're forgetting something on the island. A gift? Some kind of trinket? Maybe something that came with you to the island. You're not sure you packed your personality, but had you even brought it? You can't remember. No matter. Don't they say that forgetting something in a place just means you'll return?

Except you know that whatever you're leaving behind, it's something you'll never see again, even when you set foot once more on Keso's shores. But what was it? You can't imagine, and it hurts to think about. That's okay.

You don't need to think anymore.

Crones in Their
Larval State

detention center guard stopped Carol at the
entrance and motioned to a steel bin. "Remove
all flowers, vegetation, or silver items and
deposit them in the receptacle."

Carol brought nothing like that today. She had tried
flowers before, once because she didn't know policy and
later because she thought conditions might have improved.

But nothing seemed to improve at the detention center.
Especially not her daughter.

Satisfied, the guard let Carol into a steel hallway. Wall-
mounted plaques boasted of progress she didn't see. *In these
enlightened days, we don't burn witches at the stake. We
rehabilitate them.* After what that crone Tabatha Mbaye did
to the president, authorities had zero tolerance for
witchcraft. Anyone could be detained, even for so little as

wearing a pentacle under a school uniform. Certainly Carol agreed that witches needed monitoring, but there should've been leeway for minors just playing with powers they didn't understand.

Try telling Morgan that. She called Tabatha a hero. Teen girls thought they knew everything.

The steel hall ended at the guestroom, a humorless white square furnished with round tables and plastic chairs. Armed guards patrolled the walls and exits. Parents in ones and twos sat across from daughters in scarlet jumpsuits. Some inmates had short hair—boys or girls? Carol couldn't tell.

At the guestroom's center table sat Morgan, arms crossed, face ever petrified in a scowl.

Carol sat across from her and examined with a mother's eye. Morgan was thinner, but her bushy auburn hair was clean and her jumpsuit looked crisp, not soiled like last time. Maybe she was being polite to the guards for a change.

Not so with her mother. If Carol didn't initiate conversation, neither would speak. She cleared her throat. "So, they've started holding boy witches here?"

Morgan rolled her eyes. "Those are girls too, Mom."

"You look thin. Eating enough?"

Morgan shrugged. "It's super-processed gruel, nothing real in it. They're scared we'd use meat and veg for spells."

Wouldn't you? Carol almost asked, but Dr. Brunwick had warned against instigating. Carol forced a polite smile. "The doctor said you might be released if you'll behave, show progress. They just want to see your head's in the right place."

"I won't behave for them." A smile lit Morgan's eyes. "And I don't want to show them progress. It's mine to keep."

"But wouldn't it be nice to come home? See Dad?"

"Dad can see me whenever he wants."

Which was never. "And school? You could catch up with Rhonda and Claire." Stoners, both, but Carol would take them over the alternative.

Morgan's face softened and then turned stony again. "They'll get by. I have new friends now."

Carol had heard—Sati, Brooke, Tasha. She'd asked Dr. Brunwick about moving Morgan to another group with better influence, but he feared she'd be a bad apple that spoiled the bunch. Never mind how she was supposed to rehabilitate among the wrong crowd.

Daughters at other tables held hands with their parents. Some even laughed. A skinny ginger two tables away stared at her fathers and scratched her arm, antsy to be released. These other girls wanted to get better, but Morgan was so antagonistic. There was once a sweet girl who liked to sing about every animal she saw, no matter how hard it was to rhyme. She hadn't needed rhymes when she could sing about platypuses and giraffes. Some days Carol wondered if that girl had ever been real.

Morgan coughed. "I'll miss you, Mom."

Carol couldn't help smiling. Whatever had become of Morgan, she wasn't lost. "I'm not going anywhere. I'll keep visiting, always."

Morgan pursed her lips and turned away. "Sati's been eyeing the future. She's seen change. Little things here, great things outside. We're just missing a couple items to connect them."

Carol gaped. Witchcraft, even here? "But they took away your spell things—"

"Reagents." Morgan tugged at her hair. "Anyone can find them if they're desperate, even around the guards. They can't stop us from bleeding."

Her words sank through Carol just as screams overtook the guestroom.

The skinny ginger's eyes turned white. Her fathers retreated as a pale moth wriggled from her arm. Bits of skin broke into larvae, chrysalides, and then fluttering moths. The girl was melting away. She must have found a moth here earlier. That was enough a reagent for a young witch to work terrible wonders. A whooping alarm drowned the screams, and guards swarmed the guestroom.

A hand held Carol's—Morgan, reaching across the table. She seemed calm, as if she'd known a fellow inmate might burst into moths today. Brave girl. Carol squeezed her hand.

A jagged thumbnail scratched Carol's palm. Blood welled in its creases. She looked wide-eyed at Morgan, but guards were already pulling the two apart. There wasn't time to explain. Morgan tucked her bloodstained thumb inside her fist and vanished into the detention center's depths.

Carol followed the other parents out, curling her bleeding hand into a fist while she listened to their whispers. Some blamed their daughters. Others blamed the doctors for failing them. No one blamed the soulless wall plaques. *Thou shalt not suffer a witch her vices.*

At the hall's end, parents dallied in collecting personal effects to avoid the parking lot tide, but Carol was used to it. She pressed through steel doors and let the protestors' roar wash over her.

"Give back our daughters!" they chanted. "Set our daughters free!"

Newscasters used to scavenge the protests, but now they only reported on fugitive crones and nationwide witch hunts. If Morgan could, she would run away to join the wild witches. She believed in a coming revolution.

Carol gripped tissues in her bleeding hand. She wasn't sure what to believe anymore. Morgan couldn't be right about change; Carol promised herself that. Teen girls didn't know everything.

But as her car pulled away from the protestors and the loneliness since her last visit sank in, she couldn't help wondering: *What if they do?*

Hairy Jack

Cheers rang through colony ship *U.F. Providence*'s A-level when, millions of miles from Earth, Cherish Fernsbury was found guilty of witchcraft.

The crowd numbered three dozen. They and their cheering washed around Zana Guillain as they hauled Cherish from the A-level meeting room. Zana came because it was a communal hearing, and she was technically part of this community. She hadn't expected Paul Sutter's raving, Captain Adrian Miro's silence, or the ultimate verdict.

She hadn't expected the morose shock on Cherish's face.

As they hauled her toward a gleaming white corridor, she reached out for the captain's help, but he was a statue. Instead she brushed Zana's hand.

"Don't let her touch your skin," Paul hissed. He shoved Cherish away, and her pale, bone-thin hand slipped through

Zana's fingers. Paul and his witch-hunters wore white spacesuit gloves over their shirt sleeves. To handle a witch.

Zana stared at her hand. Four fingers, a thumb, the creases that street wanderer Mama Margot once called "fate lines." Zana couldn't remember her fate, only that it had felt magical when Mama Margot's gnarled fingertip stroked her skin. No boils or warts blemished her hand now.

"Wait." She was too soft-spoken, and Paul was too much in his own head to hear.

Michael Sloan broke briefly from the group. "It's okay. They'll hold her until we can string up her animal, too." He gave Zana's arm a reassuring pat. "Don't worry, you won't miss the execution." Stringing up was a relic from ancient history. Their metaphorical hangman's rope was the airlock.

But if they were waiting to catch the animal, then there was time.

Zana wasn't alone when the witch-hunters left. Adrian remained, breathing too hard to be silent. She stared at him until he noticed and raised a helpless hand.

"What can I do?" he asked. "I'm one man. If they won't listen, I have no authority."

He commanded the bridge, but would he hold a colony ship hostage over one woman? No, he would keep the ship jumping through star systems until they reached Atta.

"We're outside United Federation laws here," he went on. "That's what we wanted, a pilgrim ship of sorts. Everyone signed up for this."

Not everyone. Zana came looking for literal greener pastures than Earth. She still hoped to find them. Maybe at Atta, this barbarism would be punished proper, but too late for Cherish. *U.F. Providence* was in the hands of the few.

Adrian sighed. "Even Cherish came aboard to practice religion freely."

"Then why hurt her?" Zana asked. She was surprised she could speak at all.

"They're irrational. You won't win them over with reason."

"As with witches in Salem."

"I'm no history teacher, but if I recall, there were no witches in Salem."

"There's no such thing as witches." Likely Zana and Adrian were the only two people on this ship who knew that. "If I find the animal, I can use their irrationality against them."

Adrian wiped at his blue captain's coat. "I won't stop you." He looked like he wanted to tell her not to get her hopes up, but he walked away without another word.

Zana never pictured herself as someone who got involved. Even the religious specifications of the colony hadn't bothered her until the first whispers of witches. People found dark ages whenever they chose to make them, and the colonists found their darkness millions of miles from Sol. This might have happened on the other ships bound for

Atta. Cabin fever in space, violence, mutiny. Perhaps she was witnessing why half the ships never reached the colony.

She left A-level's meeting room through the narrow corridor where Paul and his zealots had dragged Cherish.

Dehydrated foodstuff and oxygen equipment packed the walls. There was no space to spare, even on a colony ship ferrying over two thousand sleeping souls from Earth. Zana hadn't seen its outside in months. At boarding months ago, *U.F. Providence* reminded her of the beached cruise ships she spent her childhood scavenging on the bleeding coast. They were ancient, forever overgrown with carnivorous algae that turned the coastal air red and toxic. She was lucky to have a broom put in her hand and then a meager paycheck, luckier to later be handed a free ticket to Atta. Even a holy pilgrimage needed someone to scrub the toilets.

The corridor reached an intersection. Ahead lay the A-level portside maintenance airlock. Scuff marks blemished the floor where its door slid up and down. Through its window was a compact chamber, where another door let out into infinite emptiness.

They would execute Cherish here.

Zana pictured her inside, at first banging on the door with her bony hands for sympathy and then, resigned to her fate, seated at the chamber's center. In a split-second, she would be freed of artificial gravity and life support. She would float into the void. The ship would activate the next faster-than-light jump, and then it would be like Cherish never existed. They wouldn't even give her the decency of a lifeboat shuttle.

That made Zana laugh and cringe. These marvels of human ingenuity—the CycloDrive engine's artificial gravity, renewed air and water molecules via TerraTech, and Juggernaut FTL's power to slip through ancient pathways once carved by comets. All these technological miracles, and they were about to execute a woman for witchcraft. Might as well beat her to death with clubs carved from mastodon bones.

People never changed.

A muffled, throaty bark snapped Zana from the airlock window. The animal's musty stink hit before she knew what she was looking at.

Down another empty corridor stood the black dog everyone had seen the past few days. Large and shaggy, he had a long snout and folding ears. He gave another muffled bark.

Zana snapped the multi-tool off her belt. It had a pen, a flashlight, other things, among them a blade for cutting tape and plastic. Each passenger had one, even Cherish before Paul confiscated it. Zana wasn't sure she could hurt a dog, but against the life of another human being, she might try. She stepped into the dog's corridor.

He waited until she walked halfway from the airlock and then bolted into the room behind him and around a corner.

Zana charged after him. A food cylinder clattered on the floor in front of her, scattering freeze-dried potato and mushroom pellets. The dog waited at the end, his shaggy tail wagging, taunting. She kicked past the spilled foodstuff. He darted down another corridor, where someone shouted and something heavy hit the floor. She followed the noises.

He wasn't in the next room or the corridor beyond, but he had led her to Paul. He stood outside A-level storage, while another man whose name Zana didn't know helped Michael limp to a wall-mounted bench. She started toward the next corridor, but Paul called her over.

"What's your business here? You can see the witch when we execute her."

Zana belted her multi-tool. She didn't want these men to get the wrong idea. "Have you seen a dog?"

Paul crossed his arms. "Skulking around, thinking we're idle. Michael ran after. Sprained his ankle."

Michael raised his left pant leg. The ankle looked fine, but he rubbed it anyway. "Disappeared the second I looked that way."

"You should have stayed put," Paul said. "He'll lead us astray, fade into nothing, and come back to free his unguarded mistress. It's no natural animal. Tales of scavenger dogs date to our forefathers, omens of misfortune and death, like crows with fur. Black Shuck is one, Hairy Jack—"

"Jersey Devil," Michael added.

"Well, not quite, but he has his place at the Devil's table, where beasts sup as men while men crawl on the ground as beasts. She would do his work and make us crawl this way." Paul was talking to Zana now, too, a sermon for all of three listeners. "The dog drains our luck and gifts it to her. It's no coincidence that when she's around we have accidents, malfunctions, nightmares. She'll navigate our ship into uncharted horrors."

Michael cringed. "She's sat on my chest in the dark. I wanted to get up, but she wouldn't let me." The unnamed man nodded.

"If she's so powerful, why's she a prisoner?" Zana asked.

Paul looked taken aback. Had no one asked that question? "She's isolated in space. Nowhere to go."

"And we've taken precautions." Michael held up a spacesuit glove.

The unnamed man's lips cracked open. "Faith."

Paul and Michael murmured agreement. "And we think she's put her power inside that animal," Paul said. "A trick to look powerless to the soft-hearted. That's why we have men searching. Even when she's gone, the dog might tempt another. Neither can join us in Atta. Steel your heart, Ms. Guillain, or she'll steal it."

How long had it taken him to cook that up? He talked like this was a game. Fine then, Zana could play if winning meant saving a woman's life. "Couldn't the dog alone be the trouble? It might've bewitched her." However a dog could do that. Puppy eyes? Laying his head on her lap?

"Calm down. She's just a witch. You think witches don't want to leave Earth, same as the saved?"

"I think a dog that carries witch powers might cast a spell on a woman like Cherish. I'd rather break a spell than execute her."

"You'll find the dog? But you're a janitor."

Zana marched away toward the unexplored corridor, where a ladder descended to B-level. "Then I'll clean up your mess" popped into her head when she reached the bottom. If only she'd thought it up in Paul's face.

Better than what she wanted to say, what she muttered to herself as she searched B-level. "You're evil." It was crystal clear. They weren't drugged, mentally ill, or even ignorant except on purpose. They were evil men whose brains let them check every moralizing box necessary that let them murder a woman in cold blood.

Catching the dog would uncheck some boxes. That was the only spell to break.

Zana's search continued to C-level, where machine noise filled the heart of *U.F. Providence*. TerraTech life support pumped air and water through the ship. Not far away churned CycloDrive's gravity and Juggernaut's FTL engines.

Zana passed a cramped room, where two off-duty engineers played cards on a digital tabletop inside. The black dog waited at the end of the nearby hall. He stood at knee height on A-level, but here he grew every time Zana blinked. It was not the size of animal that should be able to disappear without a trace, not something that should have boarded the ship unnoticed. He must have been smuggled.

Zana drew her multi-tool again, her thumb ready to pop the blade. Every footstep was cautious. Paul was right; the dog did make people crawl, in his way. She neared the corridor's halfway point.

"Here, Shuck. No, not Shuck? How about Jack? Here, Jack."

The dog's left ear ticked as if pecked by a fly. He looked the size of a young mule, and then a cow.

Zana froze. If he stood his ground, she would actually get near him, and then what? Stab a thing like that?

He turned from her and lumbered around a corner.

She started breathing again, hadn't realized she'd stopped. Before his tail slipped out of sight, she charged. One misstep and her multi-tool slid through her fingers and clacked on the floor. Its blade scratched her palm. Wincing, she grabbed it and reached the corridor's end.

No surprise, Hairy Jack was already gone. Witch or no witch, the dog was a chameleon, hair so dark that if he hid against a viewport, he might blend with the blackness of space. No one would catch him unless he wanted to be caught.

"What's that banging?" A bearded, middle-aged man popped his head through a door to Zana's right. His badge marked him as chief engineer.

"Looking for a dog," Zana said. It sounded ludicrous. Every pet was in deep sleep with the rest of the passengers on D-level and E-level. "Never mind."

"No, I know what you mean." The chief scratched his hairy chin. "Captain knows it, too. Bite you?"

Zana glanced at her hand. Blood gelled between closed fingers. "No, that was me. Clumsy."

"Should've figured." The chief beckoned. She followed him to a break room where he opened a first-aid kit. "Anytime it passes, our stuff goes fritzy. Bad luck when it crosses your path."

Bandages piled into Zana's clean hand. She wiped at her lacerated palm until the blood was a faded smear. The multi-tool's cut ran along one fate line. What would Mama Margot have said of that? Zana wrapped white cloth around her hand. "Weren't black cats bad luck?"

"Birds, cats, dogs. Can be black anything." The chief coughed. "Any sort of animal, that is. It's not right, the way it looks at people like it's waiting for something bad to happen. When you wait for bad things, they come. Last time, the air stuttered on D-level."

Zana supposed engineers had their own superstitions apart from Paul and his witch-hunters. Down among the clunking machinery, the chief's fears seemed more cogent.

These engines kept people alive. They could bring death, too, especially when an omen of misfortune trotted their halls on four legs.

Across from the break room there stood a door that warned unauthorized personnel to stay out. The way Hairy Jack slipped in and out of sight, it seemed a door like that would be no trouble. Yet he couldn't slip past Paul and his men. Did their faith hold the line or was the dog less spectral than he seemed?

"Can you shut off air to any corridor or room?" Zana asked.

The chief shrugged in a way that meant yes. "Doors seal it, sure." His eyes filled with understanding. "Oh. Well, sure. I'm on Com-6. You can speak to me from any wall pad."

Zana thanked him and returned to C-level's corridors. She passed another restricted door and slipped down three halls before she spotted the dog again.

He leaned his forelegs at the floor, arched his back, and then stood up and wagged his tail. His eyes were two little stars reflecting the overhead lights. He was an ugly thing, his lower jaw misaligned with the rest of his head, his matted hair mucky like he had been rolling in Earth's worthless soil. A rambunctious animal like him would love green Atta.

He wanted to play, like Paul and his zealots. The dog's game was not of murder, but the chase.

Zana squeezed her multi-tool and retreated two steps. Hairy Jack's head leaned in. She had his interest. But if she played his game, he would chase her. He could catch her. Then what?

Cherish's morose face filled her head, that mouth black and hopeless as space outside, as the dog.

Zana darted out of the corridor and across the hall. She paused only to listen. Yes, Jack was following. His were quiet steps for a dog his size, but Zana heard four paws thump closer. She took off again. To her left, a door snapped shut, open, shut again, clearly malfunctioning. Through the living quarters, she heard one engineer shout about a "damn table" and guessed the card game had flickered out at the dog's passing.

At the next corridor, she squeezed against the wall to one side of the door and chucked her multi-tool as hard as she could. It hit the floor several paces down and slid until it clacked against a wall.

Hairy Jack barreled past her. He'd grown elephantine, yet somehow slipped through each narrow opening. His stink filled the air, musty and dirty. He was every mangy dog that had escaped the urban unit at the wasteland's edge where Zana grew up and then returned a week later only to be chased off. His jaunt slowed at the thrown multi-tool, where he glanced side to side, looking for her. He wasn't the only one who could vanish.

She slipped around the doorway and pressed one clean finger to the wall pad. "Chief? Hall C-13."

The door slid shut. Through its window, she watched another door drop where the dog's nose poked at her multi-tool. He didn't notice that his game was over.

Almost over. He stumbled back from the multi-tool. His mouth hung open, that misshapen jaw disappearing in shaggy black hair, and began to hack. Zana turned away from the window and covered her ears. She thought this would be quick but wished it would be quicker.

After a few minutes, the chief unsealed the corridor. There was only a quiet stretch of floor to cross, where a prone dog lay beside the multi-tool. He would've only come up to Zana's knee if he could stand. He'd been inflated with fearsomeness and now it had died.

She prodded him with her foot. No movement. Her fingers searched inside his knotted fur for breath or heartbeat and found only soft, still flesh. There was nothing spectral to him, no legendary Hairy Jack. A dead animal, that was all.

She belted her multi-tool and wormed her arms under the body. He was lighter than he looked, built more of hair than tissue and bone. How could she have ever been afraid of an animal so frail? Paul might've blamed God for having him kill the poor creature, but Zana couldn't be Paul. She had done this to keep him from doing worse.

He, Michael, and the other man still lingered outside A-level storage when she returned. A half-dozen witch-hunters had joined them. She knew their names and faces, but she didn't feel like greeting them. She looked only at Paul.

He was beaming. "You found him. What did you do?" His smile grew when Zana explained the trap.

"Strung him up," Michael said, resting his leg on the wall bench.

Zana hefted the dog's body. "There's no need to hurt Cherish now."

The men glanced at each other and then at Paul. He closed his eyes. The smile stayed. "Ms. Guillain, she's a witch. What transpired between her and the dog is God's business. We only work his will. Whatever her power, we mustn't suffer a witch to live."

Zana's fingers curled inside the dog's thick fur. Even with the symbol of their superstition dead, they weren't going to let Cherish go. "Evil."

Paul raised an eyebrow. "Pardon?"

"I want to see her. I want to show her it's dead. After that, do what you want."

Michael started. "It's not what we want exactly—"

Paul raised a hand. "Please don't take this as ingratitude. As I said, you'll see her at the execution. Why not rest until then? You've earned it." He reached for the dog's body.

Zana held tight. The dog's musty stink coated her shirt. "I killed him. Alone. You're going to doubt me? Why do you want him so bad?"

Paul recoiled. All of them did, even Michael in his seat. They were so irrational that she could fix her words and point the finger at any of them, name him witch. But she couldn't be Paul.

"I will see her." Zana approached the storage room. No one stopped her. The door slid up to the ceiling and closed behind.

Cherish knelt on the floor. She hadn't been praying, only dozing. She looked ill-suited for travel even before being taken prisoner. Her clothes hung loose on her bony frame, and auburn hair tumbled around her gaunt face. That face would haunt Zana long after Cherish slipped out the airlock, the dog's body being her only companion. Paul and his witch-hunters would forget. The colony would be none the wiser.

Zana would remember. She couldn't help it. She knelt, still clinging to the dog. "I'm sorry. I tried."

Cherish reached beside Zana's face and tucked a red curl behind her ear. "No, dear. You did exactly what I needed. Open up, Jack." Bony hands explored the dog's hairy head and snout. Cherish pressed two thumbs against the corners of his mouth, and his jaw slopped open as it had when he was desperate for air. She dug past tongue and teeth, into his throat, and yanked out a wet, emerald-colored bauble. Jaws snapped shut behind her fingers.

Zana stared into her sunken eyes. "I don't understand."

"You don't need to understand." Cherish popped the bauble between her lips. It made a bulge at her neck as it descended her throat. "Put him on the floor and hand me your multi-tool."

Zana did as she was told. "But I wanted to save you."

"And you have. You brought my Jack back to me. The chief engineer doesn't hate me, might've been fine, but you have a soft heart. You're perfect." Cherish dug the multi-tool blade into the dog's fur. There was no blood underneath, only deeper hairy layers, as if Jack was built only of shaggy blackness.

"Paul was right?" Zana asked.

"Paul talks too much," Cherish said. "He's bound to say something true now and then."

Zana flexed her hand where Cherish's desperate fingers had stroked hours ago. "But there's no such thing as witches."

Cherish's thin lips curled into her cheeks. "They only wish I was something so nice as a witch. They wish I served so kind a creature as their Devil." She threw the dog's hide around her shoulders like a shawl and stood from his still-hairy body. "Leave Jack in my place. He's right where he needs to be."

"Where are you going?"

" *We* are headed for the lifeboats. Lead us."

The storage room door slid open. Zana treaded reluctantly, Cherish right behind her, ready for Paul to accuse her of aiding a witch. They didn't look at Zana. No one noticed Cherish. She was a specter, as if they had stared at the stars beyond and dreamed up someone to hate.

Zana might've steered toward the captain's quarters or the bridge, but each time she thought it, Cherish touched her hand. If she was bewitched, shouldn't there be a sensation? Nothing felt different inside. She wanted to reach the A-level shuttle bay. She just knew she shouldn't.

"I can't fly it," Zana said as the bay door opened. "I don't know how."

Cherish took the lead. "I worked the bridge, helping navigation with the Juggernaut jumps. Did you know that?" Zana didn't answer. Cherish had been one of the captain's own personnel and yet he wouldn't help her. Why had Zana ever boarded this unholy ship? Her one shot at a better world had become a nightmare.

Cherish climbed inside the lifeboat nearest the bay's airlock. Zana followed without protest. A few dials and switches flicked, and the lifeboat chugged to life with air and power. The interior bay door slid shut.

"If it hadn't been for Paul, I wouldn't have had to put you and Jack through that nonsense," Cherish said as the airlock opened. She guided the lifeboat through the slender exit, where it floated free of artificial gravity, FTL travel, and the rest of *U.F. Providence*'s resources and people. "They would never have noticed me slip away, but now? There's no green place for them. We've let loose Hairy Jack.

There's no more dangerous a death omen than a dead one. Watch."

Zana again did as she was told. Through the lifeboat window, she watched *U.F. Providence* shrink against the starlit universe. She saw it better than she should have at this distance, as if through ghostly eyes that explored the ship. They slid to C-level, behind doors unwelcome to the living.

"Hell is Earth, and Earth spat up the Devil," Cherish said. "Now the Devil dies."

"Do you have to hurt them?" Zana asked. Her voice was small.

"It's not up to me. Jack won't let them follow us."

Life support died for D-level. The chief and his engineers scrambled, some at the C-level controls, others descending in spacesuits to D-level to make manual repairs. It was a distraction. They were too scattered to notice when CycloDrive made a discomforting rumble. When Juggernaut roared to life, it was too late. They were busy screaming.

CycloDrive reached through the ship's cramped rooms and narrow corridors and hugged everything it touched. Walls sucked together; ceilings kissed floors. The outer shell crushed *U.F. Providence*'s skeleton, the ship's hard molecules fusing with soft flesh inside. The artificial gravity should never have been so strong, but CycloDrive was malfunctioning. It showed restraint only toward Juggernaut.

The FTL engine powered up for one final jump before it joined CycloDrive's compact new form.

Ravenous space opened its maw where unfolded a cosmic throat. *Providence*'s crumpled bow slipped inside. The maw swallowed the ship. Its bits and pieces must have scattered meteor showers across a hundred systems.

At last, the lifeboat was alone.

Zana's face sank into her hands and the bandage scratched at her cheek. A thin hand squeezed her shoulder.

"Why so upset?" Cherish asked. "You helped me; that's what you wanted. Could you have really been happy with those fanatics? Would you have jumped into the airlock with me and Jack?"

Zana swallowed a sob. "We're isolated in space. Nowhere to go."

"No, dear. We're right where we need to be." Cherish pointed at the starry universe. "Each time a ship passes through, we've snuck away to our shrouded home."

Zana lifted her head. "Atta?"

"There is no Atta, not like they believed. Too Earth-like. But there's a green place for us. Our guide will show the way."

Cherish slipped the dog's hide from her shoulders. It piled in layers across her lap, gaining shape as it fell, until it grew into the hulking, shaggy beast Zana had chased through *U.F. Providence*. He licked furiously at Cherish's face, making her giggle and squeal.

She cupped her hands around his head and rubbed his ears. "Who's a good boy? You are, that's who. My Hairy Jack's a good boy." His tail wagged until he turned to the windshield. Cherish looked with him. "Best forget Atta. Forget space age puritans and Earth ideals. The blood's been spilled. You can live. Wouldn't that be nice, to just live?"

An eyelid of space slipped away from an emerald-colored world. White wisps painted its atmosphere in healthy clouds. Zana saw its surface better than she should have at this distance, as if she already walked its clean coasts, lush fields, and flourishing farmland. Men and women tended to crops with tall stalks that Zana could almost grasp with her bandaged hand. Beyond spread a forest where dogs and children played, no wasteland in sight. As if they could see her watching, their faces turned skyward. They seemed peaceful, their eyes filled with laughter. Why wouldn't they be? Whatever they had done to reach this place, they were here.

Cherish looked expectant. Zana nodded.

The lifeboat sped toward the green world, led by a strip of space with a wagging tail, black and hairy as a dog.

Daisy

D aisy encountered the boy years before she found him smiling in the barley field. She was minding her business in a store's lot at town's edge, poking at garbage that might hide treasures. A dirty, skinny little thing, not so different from her, the boy toddled out of the store holding the hand of an older woman. This was the morning Daisy could not forgive.

"Look, Aunt Delia!" he shouted. "A puppy!"

Daisy was young and small, but she hadn't been called a puppy in a while. She approached the boy.

Aunt Delia bent over, hands on both knees. "Isn't she cute? That's a yellow lab. Her hair's almost tawny as yours." She reached into her shopping bag.

Daisy's ear perked at the sound of tearing plastic. Yes, there was treasure here.

"Your mom won't mind if we share a little." Aunt Delia reached out, a piece of sweet-smelling meat in her hand.

Daisy hurried to devour it, and then licked the residue off Aunt Delia's palm. She didn't tremble when the boy's chubby fingers stroked the fur across her head. These seemed like decent people.

"Isn't it funny how some people look like their dogs?" Aunt Delia asked. "Such a happy girl. I bet her owner looks happy, too."

The boy smiled around a missing tooth. "I want to look happy." His petting hand curled into a tiny, tugging fist, its fingers clenched around Daisy's left ear. "My puppy!"

She yipped and darted back. The boy was still smiling, the dark gap in his teeth telling her to run before he did something worse than yank her ear. She dashed home, fast as she could, where she hid.

And waited.

She found him again in the withering barley field near the old railroad tracks, where conifers marked the line between town and lingering wilderness. Years had left her young, but wiser. He was older, but still the same. She recognized him by his hair likes hers, by the gap where a tooth had been knocked out or never grew, and by the vicious smile around that gap. He was no longer a small boy, but a lanky man, smiling through tears. He was in some kind of trouble, but proud of it.

Daisy scratched at her ear and barked once. He looked at her. Then his face brightened and that gapped smile widened, as frightening now as outside the store years ago.

She ran. He chased her.

It was easy. He had a shambling gait, his shoes ill-fitting. His body seemed out of shape while Daisy's was ever strong as she wanted. She kept just ahead of his grasping hands. Mouthy, he called to her like she would stop if he talked enough.

She led him around the barley field a few times, to tire him, and then took off down the slope and across the overgrown railroad tracks toward home.

His footsteps paused when they reached the dirt trail. It winded around reddened maple trees and yellowing underbrush to a small wooden stoop beneath a half-open doorway. Nature had retaken this place and left only one narrow house, built of aged and water-soaked wood, its windows aglow with friendly firelight.

Daisy looked back at the man who had once been an ear-tugging boy. The setting sun painted the sky red behind him and a shadow fell across his face. Something had spooked him out of mindless want.

What a greedy creature he was. He was hurting, she guessed. If she became his, went home with him, she would not make him happy. His pain wouldn't end. Possessing her would only change her into a thing like he was—petty, listless, demanding—and then, yes, his dog would look like him.

But she didn't belong to him. She wagged her tail and squeaked out an encouraging yip. That snapped him out of caution. He started giggling, and the chase carried down the trail, up the stoop, through the open front door.

Daisy followed the warmth and the smoky scent along a short hallway and around a corner to the library and its fireplace. Her mistress's chair, cushioned with red velvet, sat to one side of the doorway, unseen from the hall. Bookshelves lined every wall, their volumes plump and well-read.

The lanky man popped through the doorway, still giggling, his sweat cutting lines down his dirty face, when a hand swung from around the chair and grasped his outstretched arm in long, gnarled fingers. There was no chase left in him and even less fight.

He didn't look at the chair right away. His gaze fixed on Daisy, his eyes reflecting where she sat ahead of the fireplace, at the foot of her mistress's seat. It was almost as if he'd caught her in that puzzled gaze, his happy puppy.

Her eyes grew large and red. Damp, her tongue stretched to the floor. Her features twisted in the shadows cast by the dancing firelight until she looked more her age, a wizened, haggard creature with hungry eyes and sharp teeth. She yipped once more, this time guttural and deep.

From the chair came a heavy chuckle. At last, the man turned from Daisy to her mistress.

Daisy reflected on Aunt Delia's quaint observation. But likely her nephew didn't think it was funny how some people looked like their dogs. Not funny at all.

The Umbilical Chord

I don't know where she found the Walkman. The tape should have been harmless by virtue of obsolescence. Yet there was Beatrice, pink pastel headphones over her ears, Walkman clipped to her swaying skirt's waistline, the black audio cassette grinding its gears. One hand swept a pencil as if guiding an orchestra.

I tackled her and ripped the headphones off. Ripped out a few hairs, too. Her red, teary face twisted in protest, but I didn't explain. Best there was no need, that I'd taken the tape before she heard enough of the song. That evening, a bulge formed at her belly. I'm not the kind of mother who would point that out and prayed to you that it was normal bloating before her monthly visitor.

But it was too late. The next afternoon, her school spammed me the same text over and over: PICK UP

BEATRICE IMMEDIATELY. When I arrived, she staggered across the parking lot, hands clenched to her ballooning gut. I would've put her at five months pregnant if I didn't know better. The school nurse's lips rained fire and brimstone. You'd think a Catholic school of all places might be sympathetic to a pregnant virgin.

"Mommy, it hurts," Beatrice signed so I could understand. Her wincing face was a sloppy mess, too distraught for me to read her lips.

I hugged her, cleaned her up, and took her home to my office where I'd locked the cassette tape in my roll-top desk. That had been its prison since long before she was born, yet she'd crossed paths with it before. It had ways of making itself found. Like when we were kids and played in the woods. It drew us towards it. Soon enough Marianne spotted the burn barrel beside the tree. Johnny dug up the tape, intact among its ashes. You had an old Walkman. We didn't need our mother's negligence for the tape to haunt us.

I couldn't throw it away after everything that happened. Some other innocent gang of kids might have found it, given a listen. That, and another reason.

Retrieving Beatrice's Walkman from the bottom drawer, I would've blasted the song at a packed football stadium to spare my little girl. Her finding a means to listen had only been a matter of time. And now she had to listen again. "Hair of the dog," I signed, and then jammed the tape into the Walkman. You, Marianne, and Johnny took turns with your headphones while I watched, angry and envious over being the deaf girl. I didn't know then that I'd never been so lucky to be left out.

I watched as the song slithered into Beatrice's ears. She breathed in, out, and with each exhalation her belly shrank. I felt you watching, disappointed as the summer of '92 echoed in our heads, decades later. We both felt that thing's presence inside your niece. I shot frantic emails to every unsavory doctor my firm had ever represented. Like you and the others discovered, relief was fleeting.

Tuesday morning brought Beatrice a first trimester bump. She listened to the tape before breakfast. She listened again when she came home that afternoon, and again at bedtime. The whole day, I felt you pacing behind me. You think it's my fault, don't you?

By Thursday, the Walkman joined Beatrice at school, where the tape eased the bloat between classes. The same song and dance we'd seen before, except you told me no one would ever dance to "those miserable violins." No worry she would break it; it had survived Marianne's scissors and Dad's power drill. Even unspooled by Johnny, it collected itself. Too many dead kids had tried their best. Beatrice never asked why listening to the tape started this or why re-listening helped. Sweet girl, taking mercy on her shitty mother who let this happen. It's not as if you and I ever had any answers.

Dr. Clark reached out on Friday and agreed to perform the unscrupulous surgery that might save your niece's life. I was packing bags when she came in, eyes wet and red. A boy on the school bus had snatched her headphones off and slapped them over his ears. She grabbed them back, but by then he'd heard the song.

"Can we save him, Mommy?"

I remember when you tried to copy the tape, give the others relief, but said when you played them back the blank cassettes had filled with inhuman screeching. Then Johnny tried to steal the original. I still have the scars on my back from his father's box cutter. He was so angry after Marianne died and thought better to go after me than you. I was the smallest, but I alone was immune to our gang's musical curse. That somehow made it my fault.

I lied to Beatrice. Told her the tape couldn't hurt boys. We left for Dr. Clark's, spent Friday night at a motel, where she took the headphones to bed. By Saturday evening, our hometown news discovered the boy's fate. Spontaneous human combustion, they called it. Some journalism major will theorize our town is prone to that if they ever look back on Johnny's headlines.

Somewhere close, they'd soon find another body, its condition harder to explain away. Same as Marianne's mother, Johnny's father. Same song and dance.

Near midnight, we parked outside the storage unit/illegal-as-hell clinic, every corner stuffed with stolen medical equipment. Dr. Clark was greasy and untrustworthy, like a used car salesman, but we were out of time. I laid Beatrice across the surgery table and hugged the pink headphones over her ears. She asked if she would be okay. I promised she would and stroked her hair until the anesthesia machine coaxed her to sleep. Dr. Clark slid one ear free and went to work with silvery instruments.

She was so peaceful.

Not like when you lay screaming on our bedroom floor, a sharpened pencil in my reluctant little fist. "Do it, Donna!" you screamed. "Get it over with!" Your belly was already bulging again. We never got the chance to see if our way would've worked.

In the storage unit, Dr. Clark's gleaming scalpel clattered to the floor.

Beatrice's gut swelled free of the sheet, and a palm pressed up beneath the skin. I squeezed the headphones over her bleeding ear, but that was no longer enough for the thing inside. Her writhing ragdoll body knocked Dr. Clark over and slammed the anesthesia machine into me. My head banged the table's edge. The world went black.

Black as your blood when I tore the graphite pencil from your inner ear. One down, one to go. We thought it would be easy to save you, make you be like me. But then it was too late, and instead of me and you in the room, there was me and it.

I awoke in the storage unit, head aching, a familiar, coppery stink haunting the air. Beside me lay the overturned surgery table, facing away, where Beatrice's small feet stuck out from the bottom. Dr. Clark stretched beyond, his head leaking onto the cement floor. I crawled across a dark, sticky pool of sharp instruments and peeked around the foot of the table.

She's like you now, hollowed out, wrapped in my arms, fingers sinking into blood-drenched skin. But unlike you, she's already cold.

I should've been left alone to grieve back then, and now too, but a dark, daughter-sized shape watches me from the far corner. Beatrice's pink headphones grip its skull, and her blood coats its relaxed, reptilian smile. When it tore from your body, that smile promised we would meet again.

And here we are. Still think it's my fault? You're right.

You know why else I kept the tape. Those adolescent days I walked with headphones clapped over my ears to tell everyone "leave me alone," the tape inside, ready to play, to punish them if they bothered me. "Why's a deaf girl need headphones?" they asked. They'd listen, lose interest, leave me, and that thing would carve its way through them to hear its favorite song. Angry at the world for taking you, I thought I deserved revenge.

But that thing and its smile crept across time to make me pay for it.

For now it's pleased with its lullaby, but soon its skin will cool. Then it'll try to burrow inside my warm flesh, back to the dead place that treats people as pathways. It crawled onto me while I still held your body, teeth and nails tearing at my guts. The scars have never faded. I jammed the bloody pencil through its eye, forced it to find other flesh to tunnel through.

But here on the concrete floor, blood seeping into my eyes, clutching what's left of my daughter, I can barely lift the scalpel. If you're really here, stop judging and blaming me, and give me strength. Before it crawls across the floor again. For me. For your niece.

For revenge.

We All Scream

S hareen stood indeterminate in the mall's dead-end
hallway, ladies' room to the left, men's room to the
right. Long fluorescent lights flickered overhead
while she counted the seconds until she would explode. A
woman trundled out the ladies' room. She clutched the
forearm of a small boy in one hand, a same-sized girl in the
other, both their round faces shrieking through tears.

It was so easy for them. Shareen was thirteen now. Past
time to grow the hell up and step inside the right restroom.
The ladies' room mirror reflected empty sinks in the
shrinking gap of the closing door. If Shareen hurried, she
could be in and out of a stall without notice.

As her hand hit the door, another curled around its rim
and pulled it inward so that a brick wall of a woman filled the
doorway. Her eyes slid snaillike down her nose. "I think you
want the other one. There are rules, young man."

Shareen clamped her teeth across her bottom lip. "I don't belong in there," she wanted to say, as if she might come unmoored from the universe should she go somewhere she didn't belong. But nothing she might say would change this woman's mind. She was a wall, and Shareen was a child.

A bearded man in flannel swept out of the men's room in a hurry, where these sinks, too, appeared empty. Shareen caught the door. She wouldn't cry in front of this woman. She didn't dare.

The door slid shut behind her, and its quiet click cast an echo through the empty men's room. Shareen wished she had told the wall woman to piss off. She wouldn't have followed lest she break her own bigoted nonsense rules.

Shareen's teeth remained latched to her lip. She hadn't told anyone to piss off in years, not since her grandfather threatened to chop off her wavy black locks. They now drooped past her shoulders. Her mother made him leave and her apologize, saying she should respect her elders even when wrong. They often were. That was around the last time she set foot inside a men's room, but her mother or sister had always joined her in the ladies' room. She'd never had to go in alone before.

Porcelain urinals sprouted like alien pods from the peeling tan-painted wall and breathed a urine stench through the stuffy room. The stalls hung open opposite them without shoes beneath their corroded doors.

Shareen started toward the stall at the end, near the narrow window high on the wall. Bright summer sunshine glared in the glass. Farthest from the entrance would be the least used. Better that no one peeked under the first stall door and saw her flats and skirt.

Best if no one came in at all.

She was about to step inside when the plinking notes hit her ears, a giant music box playing "Pop Goes the Weasel." It made her pause, even smile, before she heard glass squeak under a hand.

The mall's lower floor sat partway below the elevated parking lot, which put the restroom windows level with the baked blacktop. A man on hands and knees stared through the glass. His tight-lipped smile crossed most of his face beneath round, black eyes. Behind him rumbled a faded pink and white ice cream truck, the source of the music.

A chill ate into Shareen's bones.

The ice cream man slithered through the underside of the window. His black shoes landed with a click. Two feet taller than Shareen, he dressed in a white uniform under a white hat with black visor that reminded her of a milkman she'd seen in an old movie. He'd been cut from a vintage magazine and pasted into the mall men's room by clumsy hands.

She meant to rush into the stall and lock the door, but now he towered over her, smiling. "Are you supposed to be here, young lady?" he asked in a pinched transatlantic accent.

Shareen's teeth scraped the word from her tongue. "No."

"That's dandy. I'm not supposed to be here myself, but I won't tell if you won't." The ice cream man's smile shrank half an inch. "Uh-oh, I've made you uncomfortable, haven't I? Gee, must've left my manners in the truck. I'm terribly sorry."

Shareen's family squabbles often ended when her sister or aunt offered everyone to start over. No excuse to hang onto a bad morning by the afternoon, they reasoned.

The words came fighting, fished from her lips by the ice cream man's smile. "Let's start over. Clean slate." She couldn't have tried that with the wall woman, whose face said she never apologized to children.

The ice cream man's smile widened. "Of course. A do-over." He raised his hand beside his ear and bobbed it to the music. At the titular *pop*, he snapped his fingers.

Shareen stood alone in the restroom. No one stared in the window. She pushed into the stall and slid the door's cold steel lock into place. It hadn't been real. Odd for a grown man to slip inside the restroom through the window; odder for any adult to apologize to her. She'd never before had to go so bad that she hallucinated.

She hurried to wash her hands at the sink before anyone real could enter and had to pump three soap dispensers to get enough. The sink water stopped just as the ice cream truck's music hit her ears. *All around the mulberry bush, the monkey chased the weasel.*

Black shoes clicked across pavement and slid through the restroom window, the tail of a white snake that coiled and then stood on browning tiles. The ice cream man waved a jaunty hand. "That's better. Now, what'll it be, Shareen?"

She wanted to say she'd never told him her name, but all that sputtered out was, "I can't."

"Oh, hogwash." His hands slid to his knees as he leaned over her. "Lay it on me. What's your poison?"

It came as if rummaged out of her purse. Or her stomach. "Vanilla with hot fudge. But all I got is a quarter."

"Twenty-five cents? Why, one of them vanilla cones with hot fudge only costs a nickel. Twenty-five cents could buy you all the ice cream you want!" A shiny quarter gleamed in his hand. Shareen didn't remember giving it to him. He danced it between his fingers as he returned to the window, his clicking shoes throwing empty echoes across the tiles.

"Why?" Shareen's one word felt like pushing a mountain.

He half-turned to her. "I'm a simple man. It's my bread and butter to feed people ice cream." He pinched his black visor between thumb and forefinger and tipped his hat. "And now, I will." His body slapped wet across the wall, where it became slimy lumps of melting ice cream and slid through the crack beneath the window. Only the vanilla stain on the tan paint said he had been there.

To run when he was bringing her ice cream would have been disrespectful. Might as well shriek and cry like that little girl whose mother dragged her out of the ladies' room minutes ago. Or hours. Time had given up on Shareen.

Why weren't kids crowding a noisy ice cream truck in a mall parking lot on a hot summer day?

The ice cream man melted down the wall and reformed from shoes to hat. He held out a wafer cone, capped by two scoops of white ice cream, their surfaces bleeding black fudge. Wax paper circled the cone to catch any drops.

"As promised." He passed the cone into Shareen's hand.

Cold crawled down her fingers. She looked the cone over like she wasn't sure what to do.

"Go on. Eat."

Ice cream leaned toward her mouth. Its sweet fudge scent mingled with the urinals' stink as a vanilla-flavored chill ran from teeth to spine.

The ice cream man hunched again, black eyes grown large as his smile. "Keep going. I want to see you enjoy it. There you go. It's a good one, isn't it? Make sure to get that runoff down the side. There's a good one. Mm."

His voyeuristic glee made eating ice cream feel dirty as licking the tile floor. She had dreaded someone might need to use the men's room. Now she wished for nothing else. Why hadn't anyone come inside? She didn't belong here, and that had unmoored her from the universe after all. The restroom was its own cosmic corner, welcome to only

Shareen and the ice cream man. If there was a third presence, it was his smile.

Her tongue nudged the second scoop. It rolled over the rim of the cone, past her hand, and plopped thick onto the floor. Its subtle echo shivered up the walls. Vanilla and fudge streams trickled together in the grimy slits between tiles.

The cone was empty. She could leave.

But the ice cream man was already bending over. "Oopsie-doodle. No trouble." He scooped the lump with one bare hand and laid it back on the cone. His breath puffed across the grungy cream. "How about I fix it?"

"Okay?" She didn't mean it. It wasn't her word.

"A do-over." The plink-plink music outside almost formed its lyrics. *The monkey thought 'twas all in good fun*—the ice cream man snapped his fingers.

Shareen's cone held two vanilla scoops again, the fudge still hot and runny. She had to start over.

"All better. And you have even more to eat. Getting your money's worth."

He wouldn't let her speak. Her jaw would only open if it meant sliding the filthy ice cream onto her tongue. She shook her head.

The ice cream man's smile froze while his head cocked to one side. "Don't be a wet rag. It's a special delivery, sold at a special price, for nobody else. Finish it. There are starving kids who'd love a teaspoon of ice cream, but I brought two whole scoops just for you." His hand, still sticky with cream, took her shoulder.

She spoke through a clenched jaw. "Have to go."

"You? Have to go?" His smile grew mean in ways she felt but could not see. "Are you going to blab about me? Don't do that, not now, not years from now, not ever. If you tell anyone, ice cream will melt out of your mouth. Everyone will say, 'Shareen, you slob! Look at the mess you've made in your hair, your clothes. It's everywhere!' You'll never clean it all up. The stain will stay forever."

She thought in rivers of vanilla. "Too much ice cream. My sister's waiting. She can help."

His black eyes grew hungry. They were only pupils now. "Sister? Your sister? Well gee, why didn't you mention sooner? A sister, hoo boy! Drag her in, Shareen. I want to see her eat ice cream." His hand turned Shareen to the door.

The hallway dazed her, its floor a raft on unsteady vanilla whitecaps. The fluorescent lights flickered faster than before, shuddering at the mall crowd's dull roar beyond the restrooms. She flung her ice cream cone at the door across and plowed through. No wall woman stood sentry now.

The closing ladies' room door cut off the mall's bustle. Beside the garbage bin, an empty tampon dispenser distorted Shareen's reflection in its steel gaze. The dandelion yellow-painted room was even stuffier than the men's, but someone had the good graces to spray mint-tasting air freshener in the last hour.

Shareen staggered into the nearest stall and kissed her knees to the cold tile at the toilet's base. Grainy residue clung to her legs. She leaned over the bowl and stuck one finger down her throat. It tasted like fudge.

Ice cream spilled up her throat, giving truth to the ice cream man's threat. Something about the mix of acid and cold suggested people shouldn't be eating this stuff in the first place. Would it be like that always?

Quaking, she crawled up the stall's wall. The toilet's auto-flush carried the ice cream's remains to places unknown, but not all of it. There was still some in her stomach, quietly becoming fuel for her cells. The sink's hot water on her hands and lips couldn't wash that away.

It came as she patted her hands dry down her skirt, a music box's song of monkeys and mulberry bushes. A simpler world, with no ice cream man.

He was back, but not as he had been. A face like a flattened ice cream cake smashed against the window, its features spreading in a melting mess. His smile came cruel and twisted at its corners. One fudge eye slid to the side; the other fixed on Shareen.

"Clever Shareen. Devious Shareen. That's a place I can't go, but you'll have to come out sometime. And I'll be waiting. This is my world, Shareen. I only let you live in it."

The ladies' room chilled, an ice box set in the back of the ice cream truck. A noise filled the room, louder than music—the wet slop sound of spilling ice cream. It flowed from faucets, up drains, over toilet seats, and down the tampon dispenser. When she left, he would be there. He would always be there, the inside of her stomach stained with ice cream like the ladies' room door. She couldn't vomit him out of her life.

Her teeth clenched. They wanted to eat her face so her eyes would not see him anymore. Wouldn't that be disrespectful? "Clean slate. Please?"

The ice cream man's smile dribbled hot fudge across the window. "A do-over? Oh, I love those. Come to the men's room, Shareen. Come back where you don't belong."

The slopping noises stopped. He was right. She would have to leave sometime. When she pressed open the ladies' room door, stained by her thrown ice cream cone, she was not surprised to see the ice cream man in the hall. He was composed into a man's solid shape again, hands clasped behind his back, a sentinel to ward her from the rest of the mall. His smile was a silent line, no dribbling, no weakness. Beneath the flickering fluorescent lights, she thought there might be another shape to him, one she felt but could not see.

Her hand pressed open the men's room door. "Pop Goes the Weasel" reached the climax of its every stanza. *Pop.* Fingers snapped in the hall.

Over her shoulder, there was no ice cream man, no thrown vanilla cone. The glaring wall woman was back, oblivious that she'd tossed Shareen into a vanilla maelstrom.

She had to go again, the pressure inside as bad as when she first stepped inside the men's room. Its door slid shut behind with a quiet click. The urinals once again breathed their acrid stink. Beneath the window, the farthest stall beckoned her to enter before she exploded.

The ice cream man stared through the glass, and his truck's music guided him down the tan wall in a melted mess. His play had restarted, the stage reset, but Shareen couldn't remember her lines. Words wouldn't come unless he wanted them. In his dull eyes, her mouth was only a means for eating ice cream.

"Let's recap," he said. "We've talked about politeness, about blabbing. Looks like all I need is your order."

He hunched, hands on knees, leaning his smile closer. The smile knew what kind of ice cream Shareen used to like but asked anyway. It needed to hear her say it. And nothing else. No more tricks, no more do-overs. The next lick of ice cream would stick inside her forever.

"Lay it on me, Shareen. What's your flavor? Twenty-five cents. That's an awful lot of ice cream. I'll have to keep it coming so you can eat the cost."

Vanilla with hot fudge. Say it.

"Spill it, Shareen. You have to eat ice cream, or I won't go away. We'll be stuck in this pit together, you and me."

Her lips parted. The line was written on her tongue, her vocal chords, and every cell within them. Her upper lip curled back.

Vanilla with hot fudge, he wants to hear it, so say it.

"Maybe you'll keep me so long that I'll belong here." That damn smile reached inside her. "So long that you'll belong here, too. How about it, young man?"

Her knees buckled. She was going to explode. She took a deep breath and unlatched her lip.

"*EEEEEEEEEEEEE!*"

The high-pitched scream tore up her throat and through his soft face. His smile scurried to one side, a frightened worm with nowhere to go. He raised one hand to his ear and snapped his fingers, but Shareen's scream drowned the music. Where was the pop?

He couldn't find it, couldn't even scramble away from her shrieking throat without tripping over his shoes. His body splatted against the wall and bubbled up through the window in a milky froth. He took one last look over his shoulder, his face a sludgy vanilla mess with dribbling fudge features, and then scrambled into his ice cream truck. The scream chased it out of the mall parking lot, remnants of "Pop Goes the Weasel" fading into memory.

The men's room door crept open. It was the wall woman, her jaw hanging, coming to check on the noise. Another scream burst through Shareen's lips and sent the woman scrambling into the hall. She was gone when Shareen emerged from the men's room.

One last scream threatened the edge of her throat, but only a sob erupted into her hand. The floor held firmer than when she had last staggered between restrooms. The universe was righting itself. She took a deep breath, held it, let it out, and wiped her eyes.

"It's okay," she whispered.

She pressed open the ladies' room door with trembling hands and passed the tampon dispenser toward the first stall. The only sound was the door's echo as it clicked shut. No sign she'd ever knelt here, and no one stared in the window.

But she couldn't move yet. She first had to listen for "Pop Goes the Weasel" to fade in from the parking lot and ripple across yellow walls. She might always be listening for it. There was no sure way to know it wouldn't come back or what to do if it did.

She supposed she could always scream.

The Burning of the Blueberries

The scent of burning blueberries brings me back through the years to my time with the Horned Brotherhood, its brush with something ancient, things that still haunt me years on. My senses of taste and smell dulled after the fire, but that scent stays. I first noticed when my wife tried to bake a blueberry pie and raw, ripe berries rolled onto a hot pan. Most people won't know that scent. I can smell them burning. They revive a memory so strong that I live it again.

It didn't start with the fire. It started with a dive bar. I seldom drink, my doctor says it conflicts with my medications, but it was my twenty-first birthday. There was no harm in going out someplace my friends didn't know about to have a moment to myself.

The bar was dim and smelled like its men's room. People weren't here to mingle. Depressing barflies clung to the barstools and even more depressing older men gathered in the billiards corner, desperate to attract a group of girls my age who were playing pool by themselves. Disgusting, but I didn't want to confront them and bring their attention down on me. I was more careful before the Brotherhood came into my life.

Then Marty approached the bartender and ordered a drink. He was the best-dressed of anyone in the bar, and to this day I have no idea why he stopped by that hellhole. Maybe, like me, he wanted to visit a place that his friends didn't know about.

He sat on a barstool next to me and said, "You don't belong here."

My shoulders tensed, the way they used to when a new person paid attention to me, but I shook hands with Marty anyway. I wasn't about to be clocked. "Where do I belong then?"

"That remains to be seen." Marty nodded to the corner billiards game. "What do you think of those guys over there?"

"I think they should find something better to do."

"What if I told you there's a place where a lot of men found something better to do than harass young women?"

Already I had a hunch he wasn't about to get involved in the corner situation, but the girls looked to be leaving. I flashed Marty a smile. Soon I would find out I'd passed a test I didn't know I was taking.

Marty was the assessor. "I think I know where you belong. Come along."

I should've been scared. Going to that dive bar was a bad idea, but so was leaving with him in a shared cab out of the city and into the green countryside. I spent most of the ride a nervous chatterbox who reminded himself that sometimes trusting a stranger is how people die.

But sometimes trusting a stranger is how people live.

Our cab turned off the dark road and onto the lengthy, curving drive of a pearl-white mansion. A bronze statue of a horned man stood at the center of the mansion's fountain, a fur cloak across his shoulders, hunting dogs at his sides, his face graven. The fountain water ran from a drinking horn held between his hands.

Marty paid for the cab ride and led me to the mansion's front doors. I might not have belonged in the dive bar, but surely I didn't belong here. At the time I'd never lived in anything nicer than a small apartment with four other people. The mansion could hold many more. Conversation rumbled from the far side of its double doors.

"Let me give you the tour." Marty pushed open the doors and led me into a palatial hall.

I had only seen places like this in movies, that massive stairway, the spacious parlor, grand halls that led to grander rooms. The men in conversation wore suits and drank from wine glasses. Elsewhere they sat on couches with beer bottles while a baseball game played across a television the length of my bedroom. Sometimes a man would break from what he was doing to clap Marty on the shoulder and say hello.

They paid no attention to me, yet. Mercifully.

"Is this some kind of gentlemen's club?" I asked.

"There's no kind of gentlemen's club like this gentlemen's club. We stand in the palace of the Horned Brotherhood."

The atmosphere was jovial. Marty showed me a billiards room that made the dive bar look like a pothole. There were rooms for video games, table tennis, card games, a grandiose kitchen, a gym, and much more, but the point was made before I saw even half of the mansion. The club's members wanted for nothing here.

It seemed too good to be true, and it was. But that came later, with the girl, and the secret.

"What do you think?" Marty asked me when the tour was done. "Interested?"

By then my legs were exhausted, but my face had frozen in an astonished grin. "I thought these kinds of places were more, you know, exclusive."

"Exclusive, yes, but to be homogenous is death." Another man appeared at the top of the second-floor stairs. He was older, taller than either of us, and he dressed in a burgundy suit.

Marty shook the man's hand. "Sir, this is Gabriel Jefferson, hopefully our latest recruit." Then he turned to me. "Gabriel, it's my pleasure to introduce Zachary Harvick, founder and leader of the Horned Brotherhood."

"A healthy brotherhood needs variety to survive," Zachary went on. "We don't exclude on race, nation, creed, or sexual preferences."

I couldn't help but think of the girls at the dive bar. "Only women?"

"You're bold." Zachary nodded to a nearby hall. "Women have their place here, and they're well-paid for it."

Imposter syndrome is a demon. At that moment it crawled up my spine and whispered evil in my ear, that every step of progress I had taken to be myself was written across my face, that I was transparent and found wanting, and I had brought it upon myself by bringing up women in a house of men.

But they didn't look at me that way. They looked expectant. They wanted me.

So I asked another question. "Then what's a man's place here?"

Zachary beamed. "Our one goal is to recapture the essence of the primordial masculine. The chase of beasts that lives inside every man."

"You have beasts to chase?"

He laughed. "In the woods out back. We have license to hunt year round." He went on talking about the yards, the outdoor activities, the festivities, meanwhile I was having a heart attack over dodging a bullet that had never been loaded, let alone fired.

Everyone there seemed so friendly. Even Zachary, for his oddities, had a sophisticated charm. All this pursuit of the primordial masculine, the chase of beasts—this is only normal man stuff, I told myself. I used my inexperience to rationalize away the bizarre. Too much, I found out later, but that first night I was enthralled.

It was four in the morning by the time I left the mansion. A brochure stuck out of my coat pocket all the way home, but I didn't need it. I knew that I wanted in. There were no dues. The Harvick estate provided everything. The exclusion of women bothered me, but the fact that I'd stepped right over that exclusion without question had a tantalizing allure.

To explain why this mattered so much to me at the time, before I learned the Brotherhood's secret, it's hard to describe. There's asking out a girl you like and having her say yes, there's entering the university you want, there's getting your dream job, but those aren't the same.

It's as if in that old existential parable when a man says to the universe that he exists, instead of dismissing him, the universe takes a closer look and says, "My God, yes, yes, you do exist. Congratulations."

That was how it felt to be invited to a gentlemen's club. It's not like I never had friends, but I did crave fellowship.

This was affirmation. I could wave a membership card in my parents' faces and say, "Look at it! Read it! Men, exclusively, and I'm one of them!"

It wasn't about my parents. It was the exclusivity. They saw a man and said, "That's a man we want with us." Not just any man. They saw me. I belonged with them.

Every weekend became a holiday at Zachary Harvick's palace. I watched sports, took walks on the grounds, but most of my time I spent talking about anything, everything. I even let my guard down now and then, talked about how my parents and I were estranged, but never elaborated why. There were plenty of other men with their own family dysfunctions that they were more than happy to talk about. I soaked up every story. My confidence grew. I became a social chameleon who mimicked gestures and phrases without trying.

It was the first time in my life that I realized you could get drunk without a drop of alcohol. In the same way, my judgment was impaired.

I'd overheard at some point that there was an inner circle, men closer to Zachary than others, but those rumors didn't bother me. I was happy with what I had.

Then there was the girl. She was the first woman I saw with my own eyes in Zachary's mansion. I knew there were women who came and went from the rest quarters, but we didn't cross paths. This one was an accident. I had come in from the outdoors to use the restroom and forgot my way back.

After getting myself good and lost, I saw her leave a room down the hall, escorted by Zachary and two burlier men whose names I didn't know. She was trying to wipe tears off her face and wrap a white bandage around her arm at the same time. Zachary appeared impatient. The men led her away without noticing me. I didn't follow them. Instead I slipped into the room where they had come from.

A first-aid kit sat on the floor, open. There was a sink basin on one wall and a few chairs. The room was otherwise barren.

A door stood across from where I'd entered. It was wide, metal, carved with what must have been runes. Through the gap at the bottom, a draft tugged at my ankles.

I knew then I was risking expulsion from the Brotherhood even as I wrapped my hand around the doorknob, twisted it, and found it unlocked. I told myself this was no dangerous cult. These were the nicest people I'd ever met. I'd never felt better in my life, and now I wanted to ruin it for myself.

But it was the Brotherhood that put enough confidence in me to open the door. I was a man before I joined, yes, but by then I was the man they told me I could be. Had I been thrown back into that dive bar the night the older men catcalled that group of girls, I knew I would've said something.

I had to see the Brotherhood's secret. I had to know.

The door resisted at first, but that was only the draft from the other side giving me a hard time. It opened onto a dark stairwell. I wished I didn't have to be alone to descend those stairs, but Marty was elsewhere in the mansion, and for all I knew he was already aware of this basement. Maybe this, too, was normal man stuff.

I began the gloomy trek down the stairwell, but I didn't have far to go. The black stone walls beside the stairs soon spread to form the walls of a circular cavern. The floor below was soil. A golden sunlamp in the ceiling shined down on a tree at the center of the room.

It was a twisted, leaning tree. Its trunk spread thick as ten men and its limbs were leafless. I know precious little dendrology, but this was nothing native to the region. Even now, I'm not sure there are normal trees that can grow underground. But this was no normal tree, I soon found out.

There were no chains in the tree limbs. Nothing suggested the woman I'd seen had been wronged here.

Zachary's voice cracked the basement's silence. "If you're going to set foot on the soil, please remove your shoes. We're loose with the rules above, but this is a sacred place." He appeared at the top of the stairwell. Behind him stood the same two men who helped him escort the girl from the mansion.

For the second time, I feared for my life in the Brotherhood's mansion. No imposter demon whispered doubt in that basement. I'd seen too much of a powerful man's secret.

But Zachary descended the steps with a smile and clapped me on the arm. "That boldness does you wonders. I love your initiative, Gabriel. We normally wait a while before inviting a new member to the basement, but it's refreshing to see a newcomer reach down and grasp the crucial pillar of our establishment. You've discovered the Brotherhood's destiny."

The two men left us. We took off our shoes and socks and strolled the soil around the tree.

Zachary put an arm over my shoulders and I couldn't help but smile. Many times when I was younger I wished that my father would throw an arm around me that way, just dad and son, but even to my brother, who he respected, he was a cold man. Colder, now.

"The first night you came here, I told you about men's place in the Horned Brotherhood. To recapture the essence of the primordial masculine, to rejoin the chase of beasts lost on us in a softer world. I don't wish the world to change. Change is life. I want us to be reborn. What we do here, beneath the earth, will bring that rebirth."

He led me to the front of the tree, where it faced the stairs.

"I've been fostering this tree for twenty years, watered by blood and sweat and ceremony, and it's about to bear fruit. You saw the girl, didn't you? She was upset, but we paid her to be here, and she came of her own free will. We cut her, shallow, just enough of a scratch that she would bleed in the soil. We used to only scratch the surface, but so much time has passed that I felt I must've misread the ritual, that it needed the act of masculine violence to go a step further. It needed bloodshed."

"To do what?" I asked. I couldn't imagine a reason to pay women to be cut that wasn't some psychotic fetish.

"To summon the Masculine Aspect. A forgotten god of the old world." Zachary gestured along the trunk of the tree. "For every man with the steel to join us, we draw him closer. At the time of destiny, he will erupt from the tree and charge us with renewed strength, sharpen us as his weapons, and then don his true mantle as Master Huntsman. Then, the chase of beasts, forever. We will be made avatars of masculinity in the flesh. Renewal, restoration, and glory for the Horned Brotherhood."

I must've had a look on my face that I felt he deserved at the time.

"I know it sounds wild. It is! But it's also true. We're nearly there." Zachary pointed at my chest, where scars hid beneath my shirt. "We need bold men like you, who throw themselves at the new, to help my inner circle usher the Aspect into the world. Are you with us, brother?"

I told him I needed to think about it, the wisest decision I made that day. Zachary swore me to secrecy, as many in the Brotherhood weren't ready for this knowledge, and told me to come back the next day with my answer, as that Sunday evening there would be the next ceremony.

Out of his mind, I thought, desperate to dismiss Zachary's raving. The Horned Brotherhood was a front for cultists, its surface bounty a disguise for the bloodshed below.

Still, I couldn't dismiss the fellowship or the confidence that now belonged to me. When I went home to my little apartment where I looked in the bathroom mirror, I saw everything that dissatisfied me about my face. Right then I wanted to smash the mirror.

What Zachary said was normal man stuff, right? The chase of beasts. It's in our nature to be impatient, not to wait, but to pursue. I'm a man. I could be even more of a man. I needed to be as much a man as possible.

Yes. I was with them. They could still call me brother.

I returned the next day with my answer. That night, I gathered in the basement with about fifty other brothers, the inner circle. Marty was among them and gave me a nod. Then we began the first of many rituals and ceremonies.

Most of it was harmless. We wore robes of earthy greens and browns. We sang songs in a language I didn't know, led by Zachary as he read from a book with a wooden cover, its surface knotted, with runes carved into the wood. They would pass around a drinking horn filled with wine that tasted like blueberries. I could skip out on any drink I wanted on the surface, but down here was a sacred place.

They placed it in my hand. I told myself just that little sip wouldn't be enough to upset the anti-depressants and hormones.

They were lies. I was sick the next day. Had I suspected then that it had nothing to do with my medications, that there was something special about the blueberries in the wine, something meant to prime us for the coming ritual, would I have left? I don't know. I found as many excuses to leave as I could, and then ignored them.

If a knife in my hand couldn't make me leave, nothing could. I just kept telling myself that the girls were being paid, they came to do this willingly, that we kept our instruments clean and ensured their wounds were superficial, that they were treated with respect. It didn't make the bloodletting any easier. There were still tears in their eyes and mine as well.

I asked Zachary how long this had to go on before the summoning of the Aspect.

"We plan to be ready by the spring equinox. Yes, that close. There's some debate among the brothers as to whether the date is important or merely ceremony."

Marty cut in. "Only ceremony. Our actions are the catalyst."

While the practice of these rituals was respectful, the reception afterwards was as jovial as the usual mansion activities. The rest of the brothers remained oblivious and the inner circle happily joined in their usual fun. They either believed we were on the right track or took the rituals as a silly requirement to join the most trusted clique in the Brotherhood.

That I didn't ask any of them what they thought says where my feelings were headed. Enough sickness after drinking from the horn made me wonder if something was wrong. I kept my guard up now because I didn't know who was buying Zachary's plan and who was laughing along for the ride. I was losing the bonds I'd formed. More important, I didn't want anyone to know I doubted, and if we weren't supposed to believe it, I didn't want to look like a fool.

I certainly felt like one. The more times I saw the basement tree, the more I became sure it was dead. How couldn't it be dead? It was planted underground with only a sunlamp for photosynthesis and watered only by scant drops of blood. Zachary was unhinged, and I was unhinged for joining him.

But the more I convinced myself that the tree was dead, the more I felt it staring at me. Not alive, but conscious. Aware. It took another handful of visits for me to understand why. The tree didn't matter, really. Dying, dead, irrelevant. We weren't feeding the tree.

We were feeding what grew inside the tree. That was the presence I felt.

From that evening on, I made sure I wasn't the last one out of the basement at the end of a ceremony. Still, I felt the tree watching me. Even above, it lingered, as if its roots crept through the mansion walls.

One night I dreamed I was in that stairwell, and I wasn't alone. I carried a heavy axe at my side, its blade glinting beneath the artificial sun. I kept my shoes on. The axe and I strode across the soil to the trunk of the tree, and we hacked at its front, hacked it open to kill whatever grew inside, kill it in the womb.

It was an idea. I didn't plan to do it, but I thought about it until I visited the basement the next Saturday, where a vertical crease had formed from the base of the tree trunk and up past my height.

"We're nearly there," Zachary said. "The night of the equinox, be ready."

I would have to be. It was too late to stop it. Cutting the tree open would only help the Aspect into the world, premature but still here.

Only now there was that crease to stare at me for the next five weeks. It taunted me like a mirror. "You won't leave," it seemed to say. "You want to see what's going to happen. You want to change. That's why you'll stay. You'll do everything they want you to do."

I told Zachary I was concerned. What if we performed the ritual and felt no stronger inside?

He gave me a friendly jostle. "It won't happen just on the inside, Gabriel. We're not conjuring up a good feelings placebo. We call to the Master Huntsman. He'll sharpen our hearts, true, but he'll sharpen our bodies as well. Be patient. The strength will come."

I was not comforted. Anxiety tightened my nerves as each day brought the ritual nearer.

Even after everything, I could've left, no strings. The Brotherhood wouldn't keep me against my will, though Zachary would've tried to talk me out of it.

I never gave him a reason. Despite my anxiety, I was captivated by the possibilities. Science is imperfect. It always will be. Imperfect and limited, and I can testify to that as well as anyone. All the hormones and surgery in the world have limits. Maybe it isn't like this for everyone like me, but I was always told to keep my expectations in check.

This mysticism, this frightening divinity, the destiny of the Brotherhood, to inherit the Aspect—that was beyond expectation. That was euphoria. Maybe I didn't have to see limits. Maybe I could be like everyone else.

So even as I shed blood for them, sang their songs, sipped from their horn that made me sick at night, even as my nerves rattled every time I looked at that twisted tree, I stayed. Through to the bloody end, I stayed. I wanted to see a miracle.

On the spring equinox, I did.

It was a chilly night. Only Zachary's inner circle gathered at the mansion. Fifty of us put on our robes and descended the stairwell like usual, but the basement had changed. Torches lit the ring of soil.

The torchlight played with the crease in the tree trunk. It seemed to flicker and slide, as if its shape and depth were inconsistent from moment to moment. Something stirred within.

Zachary stood before the crease, and I fussed with my robe close by. Whatever came through that opening, I would be among the first to see it.

"The Masculine Aspect is prepared," Zachary said. "The tree will be split asunder as he storms forth into our world. What blood must be shed has been shed. What time must be spent has been spent. Our sacrifices are complete. Tonight we inherit our reward." He opened his wooden book. "If you will all repeat after me, we will sing the war cry as befits the Master Huntsman so that the Aspect may assume the form which best suits him, and so we will assume the forms that best suit us."

While Zachary found his page, I wondered what ways this might go wrong. The Aspect could be enraged for having been brought here. It could change us into things we wouldn't like. It could kill us.

Zachary began to sing, one line at a time, so that the Brotherhood could sing after him. This went on for what felt like an hour. I wasn't ready to see what emerged, and at the same time I was impatient to get it over with.

We had barely finished the last syllable when a heavy wooden crack echoed through the basement. I couldn't see an opening in the tree, not right away, but on the inside it was coming apart. Another rich crack and I spotted a slight gap at the top of the crease. The Brotherhood held its collective breath. I leaned forward, ready.

The crease split open from top to bottom, a seam being spread apart with threads of weeds between the sides. Golden sap slid down the edges of the wound and a green arm of pulp and leaves stuck out from the tree's inner darkness.

"Do we help him?" Marty asked.

"Let him come his way," Zachary said.

The green pulp slithered off a slim arm. Fingers grasped the tree by its wound and pulled a form through, covered in green vines. The vines grew like hair from a green scalp, so long that they could cover the figure if she wanted. Her slender form crawled from the tree on trembling legs.

She hunched then, but if she had stood tall she might have crested Zachary's height. Roots and wiry plant matter sprawled from her backside, an umbilical cord still tied to the insides of the tree. Across her body grew small canes of blueberries and their leaves. Many of the berries fell to the soil as she took her first steps.

The mass of hair-like vines looked us over, and then the face emerged. The forehead wore the same texture as Zachary's book, a knotted and aged chunk of ancient tree. Plates of similar bark crept across the shoulders, the joints, and along the chest and thighs. She looked something like a human girl, something like a deer, all made of greenery. Her expression told me she was confused, as if she had left a party and had no idea where she'd parked her car. Probably all of us looked confused.

Her enchanting eyes, blue as the blueberries that dotted her body, caught me in her gaze. We were lucky to be there in that basement. She was the miracle. That was all I could be certain of. The tree had given birth to something that was not the Masculine Aspect. I didn't know what she was, born of that ancient tree. I'll never know. Zachary didn't know either.

There was a chorus of questions much more passionate than when we recited his mysterious songs. Who was she? Where was the Aspect? The Master Huntsman?

Zachary licked his fingertips and turned pages. Lightning slid between the brothers and through my nerves.

Maybe the green woman was the Aspect in an unsuspecting form, I wanted to suggest, but I kept my mouth shut. I knew it wasn't true.

Zachary fumbled with his book. "Perhaps I mistranslated." He turned another page. "The bloodshed of women—the blood shed by man. It's difficult. Their use of pronouns and past tense wasn't the same as ours. I may have misinterpreted the action's significance, but the blood we shed being women's blood—" He lost his words and retreated from the tree.

The lightning between brothers grew forked and spread in all directions. It cooked the air with broken promises.

I expected better from Marty. He ripped the wooden book from Zachary's hands and tossed it at the tree. It struck the green woman on the shoulder and fell softly on the soil. He might as well have thrown down a gauntlet.

The Brotherhood's rage awoke. They started shouting all at once, some of them at Zachary, others at the green woman. I slumped down and covered my ears. They weren't angry with me. They were angry at the mistake and their expectations. I told myself these things in my head, over and over, desperate to drown out the violent roar.

I couldn't drown out the scream. Or the smell.

Did Marty start it? I didn't see. Someone grabbed a torch from along the ring and threw it at the twisted tree, where it landed among the roots. A thick tree like that would take a long time to burn. The green woman fell on all fours and clawed at the earth, but the soil here was shallow, an illusion to soak up years' worth of blood. There was nowhere to go.

Zachary grabbed the next torch. Maybe he thought that when the Brotherhood finished with the green woman, they would turn on him if he didn't show he was one of them. And he'd had his expectations shattered as well. He was an old man. Likely he expected the Aspect to return him to his prime.

Would they turn on me if I didn't start hollering and crying for blood? If I didn't show I was one of them? There were a few who stood silent, but none of them looked as horrified as I felt.

Zachary threw his torch. It hit the green woman, and fire flared across her left side, along the vines and blueberry leaves. Her scream hurt my ears. Some of the men's shouts grew louder while others started cheering, all of them still angry. Zachary was giving a command. I couldn't understand him. There was too much noise and she was burning. I couldn't see clearly through the tears in my face, only the green shape and the yellow-white glow that ate at her side. That cacophonous basement was burying me.

I added to the din, another growling, shouting scream among fifty other growling, shouting men. Maybe they didn't hear me, but they saw me. I charged across the soil, ripped off my robe, and threw it across the green woman in a tackle. We collapsed into the soil together, where I patted at the flames to put her out. The smoke clouded my face and hurt my eyes, my nose, my throat. It had the smell of burning green twigs and blueberries in a campfire. I fought through the stinging until there was only smoke, no fire.

"Gabriel?" That was Marty. I didn't answer him. Zachary might have spoken next. The other men were still shouting, as if the Aspect had come to the Horned Brotherhood after all and filled them with blinding fury.

The green woman was whimpering, meek, scared, and weighed light as a small tree branch. That was good. We were leaving. They could chase me, but I was taking her away. I picked her up in one arm and she latched herself around me. Then I started to walk. Her tether snagged between us and the tree.

The Brotherhood closed in. If they suspected anything different about me then, I'll never know. They saw I wasn't one of them and that turned a knife in their guts. I didn't have the ceremonial knife on me, nothing to defend us. So, I tugged. And tugged. If I'd realized then what I was about to set in motion, I wouldn't have done any different.

Zachary didn't know the half of what he was playing with, how the tree was exactly what he said it was in ways he couldn't understand. The pillar of the Brotherhood.

I tugged one more time, which pulled the green woman loose. The tether of roots snapped back and sank into the tree. I felt the way I did the last time I went to an amusement park and the roller coaster crested the top of the hill, that sudden weightlessness, somewhat sickening, and then a plunge.

Chunks of black stone collapsed from the wall behind the tree. Everyone stopped to look, even me. On the wall where the chunks had broken loose lay a thick, scrambling layer of roots.

Another chunk of stone fell, this time from the ceiling, and it landed in the crowd. Now the men were screaming and panicking as the roots sank and the basement pulled itself apart.

When the sunlamp went out, I charged through them. The stairwell was short, and I was the only one with a firm direction. Everyone else was busy stumbling over each other in the dark. They had no purpose, while I had to get her out of there.

I found light at the top of the stairs and through the secret door, but no safety. A black fissure ran across the wall. The basement held up the center of the house, and if the basement was collapsing, the house was, too. I darted out of the side room, through the halls, desperate for an exit. Front or back, I didn't care.

A wall came down ahead of us before we reached the back door. I had to turn around and rush through the dining hall, where the floor sank to my left. Then through the parlor, past the stairs that imploded alongside me, and at last out the front double doors, into the parking lot.

The green woman clutched tight to me. She never tried to get away, never acted like I might hurt her, though she was wrapped in the uniform of the madmen who wanted to burn her alive.

There was a rumble outside, but I didn't wait to see who might make it out behind me and I didn't call a cab. I just kept running. The foundation of the mansion was a mystery to me and I had no idea whether the parking lot, the driveway, the horned man fountain, any of it might fall with the chain of dominos I'd set in motion when I pulled the green woman free.

I don't know when I slowed down. The run was hard and my shoes were buried in the mansion's basement. I think we made it to the dark road that turned off to the mansion's curving driveway before my legs realized we were safe. The city was a distant glow then, many miles to walk. I didn't have a plan except to get far enough away from the Horned Brotherhood so that it was like I was never there. Eventually there would be police, ambulances, fire trucks. I didn't want to have to answer any questions.

We didn't speak. I only noticed something was wrong with the green woman, besides her burns, when I tried to sit down after a while. At first I thought she wouldn't let go. Then I realized she couldn't. Her limbs had sprouted small digits from where the tree bark covered her green flesh. She was trying to take root in my clothes.

I pulled her away and let her roots rip at my jacket, shirt, and pants. My clothes made out better than Zachary's house. A little ways off to the side from the dark road, I laid her down in the crabgrass between two pine trees. She made a soft sound, almost purring.

Nestled firm in the soil, she closed her eyes and grew still. I sat with her and waited to see what would happen, but nothing did that night. What I knew for certain was that she was gone. I think she went back where she came from, to a long sleep inside the earth after having been briefly awoken by ignorant mortals. That's what I hope. We were only together for a couple of hours and most of it we just wanted to survive. I spent the rest of the night walking home.

That weekend I took a cab ride out toward the mansion in the effort of keeping up appearances only to find the driveway blocked by yellow tape. The news had reported the collapse already and spread it across all kinds of media. There was an obituary for the late Zachary Harvick. There were going to be many more obituaries and many more funerals for all the deaths at the mansion. Many of them deserved it.

There were a lot of people in that basement, and most of them died. We were all men down there. I had a chance to become like them. Instead, I was the only one who saw a wrong and did something about it, and that alone makes me bigger than any of them.

On the way back, I asked the cab driver to pull over. I needed to check on the green woman. If anyone else found her here, I didn't want them to hurt her. I had to make sure she was hidden.

There was no need. The plates of bark that covered parts of her skin had overtaken the whole of her, so that now she appeared as a length of womanly tree root that jutted between the two pines on the side of the road.

When I visited again weeks later, I found her covered by a flourishing green bush. Long green canes shot in all directions, overgrown with sweet, plump blueberries. If anyone disturbed her, it would only be to pick this fruit. She was safe deep in her earth.

Jormungandr's Dance

A fleeing crowd hit Kevin as he reached the bay bridge. He squeezed through, but their abandoned cars filled both lanes and made him clamber overtop. Someone moaned nearby, trapped or injured, but there wasn't time to aid them.

The worms were already too close.

Against the glowing city skyline, black pillars of night interrupted the lights where enormous worms burst through buildings. They were only twisting silhouettes from this distance, but Kevin had seen them up-close.

One minute he'd been hanging out with Jonas, and then the neighborhood went to hell. Their apartment roof collapsed under a twenty-foot worm covered in stretched-out human faces and a dozen squirming arms. Its patchwork hide spanned the spectrum of skin tones.

A worm made of corpses.

He didn't see what happened to Jonas, just ran fast as he could down their ravaged street, worms everywhere. Jonas was gone. Only Lamesha mattered now.

Kevin tried her cell. "Don't shout," he told himself, waiting as it rang. "Stay level-headed."

"You've reached Lamesha's voicemail!" her voice chirped. "Leave a message and have a magical day."

Kevin squeezed his phone. "Answer your damn phone. Are you thick-headed? This is no time to go AWOL." She was probably editing her ridiculous meditation videos while the world fell apart.

Meditation had started their last argument. "I think it'll help manage your anger," Lamesha had said.

"I manage it better without this junk frying my brain," he'd said, pointing at her yoga mat and laptop.

"This 'junk' makes me happy. I speak my will into the universe that you'll treat me like you love me."

He'd stormed out her door then, shouting his love like another four-letter word. He could've handled it better, wanted to, but she'd pushed his buttons. Love went both ways. He'd been too furious afterward to notice warnings about monstrous worms.

Now their fight seemed pointless. Nothing like the end of the world to open his eyes. She was too much an airhead to take care of herself. He had to reach her and get them both somewhere safe.

He was halfway across the bay bridge when a crooning call echoed from the skyline. Two distant worms faced each other, both far larger than his first. Their bodies swayed in a hypnotic dance, maybe a wormy mating ritual. It was almost beautiful.

But when the dance ended, their heads slammed together. Their wriggling pillars fused into one titanic worm large enough to crush the bridge should it reach out.

Kevin clambered faster over abandoned cars. He couldn't believe Lamesha was putting him through this. If she was smart, she'd have moved in with him like he'd suggested a million times. He could've protected her.

Still could. He just had to make it to her place.

The sky chattered. A helicopter swooped past the bridge and roared gunfire into the city. Screaming filled the air as bullets struck buildings and worms alike. Whoever manned the trigger didn't care. Pieces of worm fell away, black bits against city lights.

Kevin had seen the pieces up-close, too. They looked like dead people.

The titanic worm slapped the helicopter. It made a shrill whine, spun circles, almost righted itself, and then exploded across a skyscraper's side. Golden fire burst through the windows.

Kevin charged for the bridge's end. Splashing came behind him, an impossible mass having hit the bay. He made it to the street before crashing followed. No one moaned from the bridge now.

Up the block, around the corner—there, Lamesha's brick apartment building nestled between two others. Kevin ignored the scarred bricks and hurried indoors. Surveying the damage would only feed his frustration.

Her second floor unit's door lay in splinters. Living room, kitchen, everything was crushed. The bedroom wall gaped open, letting in a tepid draft. No sign of Lamesha. Her laptop rested sideways on the floor. Kevin picked it up, unsure what he hoped to find. There was a video running on repeat in editing mode. Lamesha hadn't had a chance to finish it.

She appeared onscreen, her nose puffy like she'd been crying, but she was putting on makeup to hide it. She flashed a brilliant smile. "Welcome to Online Guided Meditation with Lamesha! Speak your will into the universe for a magical day." She turned to her roommate sitting cross-legged beside her. "We're joined by Xana."

Xana waved.

"Let's get started! Think hard about what you want. Breathe in the fire, breath out the desire."

Xana breathed deep. "I'm willing egg rolls for dinner."

Lamesha laughed. "I'm willing my boyfriend peace of heart, peace of mind." After a few breaths, tears trickled down Lamesha's cheeks. She made a fist and punched the floor. "He's right. This is junk. I keep speaking, but he doesn't get better. What good's love when he makes me feel like trash?"

Xana grabbed Lamesha's hand. "I know what you mean."

"You know what pain does?" Lamesha asked. "It unites us. Someday all the broken-hearted will mob into one unstoppable body and rampage through the streets because we won't put up with this shit for one more day."

Kevin felt a change through the laptop screen as the universe shifted.

Lamesha's and Xana's hands melted into each other. Their bodies swayed in a familiar, almost beautiful dance and then merged.

And two bodies was just the start. Their flesh stabbed through floor, wall, and ceiling. Wet sounds echoed through the building. The video blipped and began again with Lamesha tidying her makeup.

Beneath Kevin, a quake tore the floor from her bedroom. He plummeted, screaming, and slammed hard against rubble, snapping his leg and spine. His scream shrank to a moan.

Still, a lengthy shape heard him and snaked through the debris cloud. Its hide pulsated, not made of corpses but horribly alive, a thousand hearts beating within its coiling mess of countless faces.

One looked familiar.

The video spoke. "Welcome to Online Guided Meditation with Lamesha! Speak your will into the universe for a magical day."

Forgive the Adoring Beast

Love kept me going even when my witch killed me, and she killed me many times.

I didn't know the shores were hers that first time. I had finished eating a creature of fire and bones and descended to the white beach to wash its blood off my hands. A morose whistle drew me along the shoreline while my fingers still dripped red.

I wouldn't have chosen to show myself that way to her, but I thought the whistle meant food. I followed it to a narrow crack between slanted stones and slipped inside, skin greased with serpent gristle. Hides of long-dead animals draped her shoulders, mementos of the old world. A small fire lit her cavern and breathed violet smoke. Its light reflected off glass jars where brown buds festered, efforts to grow things in dead soil.

Pitiful, I thought. To tear and eat her insides would be a mercy.

She growled and charged at me. "My home. Mine!"

I stumbled back, stunned. Things didn't run at me; they ran from me. I wasn't prepared. Her fingers latched around my head and dragged me outside, where she broke every bone in my body and threw me to the waves.

Recovery took days. I spent them thinking of she who had bested me—*me*, devourer of species! Worse, she had bewitched my long-rotted heart. Her hides enchanted greater than my animal nakedness, and her silver eyes— inescapable.

I crawled on hands and knees back to the mouth of her cavern and begged acceptance. She sighed, bared her teeth, and murdered me. Days later, I washed ashore and tried again. I welcomed every death, but to earn her tenderness, I'd have starved.

And I never starve.

But I could share. I found a man and woman in the southern wastelands, where they dug beneath petrified trees for subterranean fruit. Gifts.

Once they were dead, I carried them to her home. Violet smoke swept from its mouth, and my witch stared despondent at the sea. What good timing. Look at my bloody hands; what I've done to please you!

She flashed tearful eyes, then wrathful, and again broke my bones and discarded me. Black water bloated my body. I was sick for many seasons before I returned. I wished she'd eaten my gifts, but that wasn't her nature.

I tried simpler gifts then. Insects, shellfish—anything that might please her better. If she'd torn me open and feasted on my bones, it would have been a pleasure. The end of me—to be digested means no return—but we'd be one forever.

Always the same. Bones broken, cast into the sea. Before long, she wasn't angry anymore. As she was busy with her impossible task, I'd become a nuisance, typical as tide and storms. Why couldn't she understand? We two were alike in this dead world.

But I realized it was I who'd misunderstood. She was as special as me and needed a gift just as grand.

A god, perhaps? Yes, my teeth had experience with gods.

I found one sleeping atop a glistening glass plateau. Kneeling skeletons encircled it, its followers who'd starved to death in worship. It reminded me of younger days, everyone else praying and fasting while I uncovered the graves of dead gods and gnawed at their god-rotted entrails.

None joined me then, but perhaps my witch could. Had she, too, eaten of gods? We could share this one together.

I tore off its head.

Kneeling outside her home, I begged her attention. The horned head pulsed between my fingers, silver blood streaming down my forearms. She emerged with an exhausted grimace. I'd come at a poor time and looked down, ready to be broken and cast away.

Instead, weight lifted from my hands. Her hand passed over each side of the head, forcing its eyes shut, and then she snarled at me. A love snarl? "You'll do harm until I make use of you, it seems. Follow."

I stood, shaking, and padded after her. At last, my witch wanted me.

We climbed the slanted stones, where at the top stood an ivory tree that snatched the sun in its branches. She laid me between its roots.

"Rest now, little famine," she whispered.

Tender fingers coaxed me into loving sleep. We were one in that moment, and because time cannot be changed, it was forever, too.

I slept through her cracking the horn off the god's head, loud as thunder, and slashing open my side. Her nails gutted me, leaving a meaty hide. She slathered the dead god's silver blood across my skin and hung me from the tree to dry. Then she left.

She must've buried the head below; I smelled god-rot in autumn. In winter, it promised new life in the world, that though I was a wretched, ravenous beast, I had done one thing right. I swore if I ever healed, I would devour that head.

But its promise came true in a way I didn't expect—my witch returned.

When spring came, she climbed the tree, whistling the same keen tune I'd heard when we first met. Gentle hands took my now-brittle skin, crackling at every touch, and crushed it into powder. Hearty winds tore my pieces through tree branches, and at last I understood what she'd done. Witch, god, sun, and tree had transformed me into life-giving spores.

We were bringing back the world.

I despaired. My dust would bring all manner of flora and fauna, all horribly alive. Their genesis would digest me, and I would cease to be.

But then my pieces smiled together in their last memory of teeth. My witch had toiled at remaking the world. At last, her work would bear fruit. Our work. I'd helped bring her joy.

Better still, no wastelands meant no peace. When all things returned to life, such violence they would visit on each other, endless eons of bloodshed. My witch and I made this together.

If that isn't love, I don't know what is.

Among the Creatures of the Night

The night road told Melanie which routes to take. Lonesome highways and haunted back lanes, as far and fast as her canary-yellow Beetle could go, anywhere to get away from people. People meant traffic, and traffic meant slowing down, and slowing down meant he'd catch her. Her busted odometer couldn't count the miles left behind. Music tracked the time on the run through changing songs, and now her radio summoned Amy Winehouse into the car.

Melanie cast a hard glare at the rearview mirror. That shadow—him? No, just a tree that leaned over the road. She caught her eyes briefly, framed by crow's feet and dark bags. Her mother used to call her a handsome woman, whatever that meant. Melanie couldn't see it beneath the lines etched across her face. No telling what had drawn her admirer.

He was back there, perhaps a thousand miles behind her or just one. *Anywhere you go, I'll be there*, his smug grin had promised before she took off. *Got a sunny disposition about these things.* She took such promises to heart. This was not her first escape.

An orange light flickered behind her steering wheel. The Beetle needed gas; it had been gunning since sundown. She took the next exit and hoped that by the time her admirer reached this place, there would be traffic to stall him and she would be long gone.

Frozen at the off-ramp stoplight, she heard screaming. A woman in a torn green dress limped beneath a streetlight toward the Beetle. Pale, man-shaped things with drooping jaws unfolded from the dark and overcame her.

Green light. The Beetle shot forward.

"Not your fault; you couldn't have helped her," Melanie said to herself. Everyone had their pursuers, and she wouldn't let anyone into this car tonight. Only the radio rode with her, now humming out Laura Branigan. Melanie avoided glancing in the rearview mirror in case she spotted the woman again. The pale things were too familiar.

Her admirer hadn't been a regular at the café where Melanie worked, but one day he showed up in his midlife crisis-on-wheels, and then he kept showing up. He asked her out at her every shift, insisted on a yes she wouldn't give, had taken a shine to her. Too much shine—a glaring sun that would melt her if she didn't run.

Her co-workers weren't helpful. *He seems nice*, they had cooed. *Give him a chance.* That she didn't want to give him a chance never factored into it. They had liked his flirtatious heat; his shine lit them up.

Melanie was a winter girl, always had been. They couldn't understand.

She rolled into the gas station, full service, and cracked the window. The elderly worker took her Beetle's type of gas, and she handed him the day's café tips to be quick about it.

Knuckles tapped her passenger side window as he finished. She let it open a crack, and a young bearded man in a hoodie slipped her a flyer. *Beware the she-clowns*, it said. Melanie promised she would and left the gas station.

Wolves swarmed the roadside just before she pulled into her lane. She braked to let them cross, the smallest only pups, the largest grown elephantine, and watched with envy. The café girls should've formed a pack like this against her admirer. He would've strode in that first day and found them at the register and waiting tables, all snarling and barking and howling at his grin and shine. They should've sent him scurrying off faster than his car could take him, never to show his face again.

When the last wolf passed, Melanie raced again. Toothy faces flashed past her headlights and vultures lined the trees. Three yellows lights threatened in a row, their glare weighing too shiny in her eyes. Her admirer might have come from a town of monsters like this.

Red light, but only for her. Behind the Beetle's bumper, each stoplight turned green in sequence as if welcoming the shining pursuer.

Headlights stroked the Beetle's side. His top-down Cadillac rolled alongside her, radio blasting an Elvis song. They both preferred the songs of the departed. *Ain't it nice to meet a kindred spirit?* he seemed to ask. He turned, eyes hidden by black shades, face weathered by ancient sunburn, and flashed her a wicked grin. There was a shine in his teeth.

Despite every mile between here and the café, he'd closed the distance.

The café girls clambered from his backseat and onto the Beetle where they leered in the windows, their faces dolled up with greasepaint. *You're no spring chicken and could do a lot worse*, their smiles said. *It's not too late to get you painted, too.* Had he done this to them?

The Cadillac cleared its throat. They could end it here, but that would be too easy. He wasn't looking to catch her yet.

First he wanted to chase.

Green light. The Beetle shot through the intersection, she-clowns clinging to its frame. The Cadillac roared from behind. Headlights filled the rearview mirror, or was that his shining face? Melanie had only seen him in the day. At night, he became a shooting star across terrestrial highways.

Greasepaint-coated faces crowded her windshield. Clowned-up like this, Melanie couldn't tell one café girl from another. They could have looked just like her underneath, could've been her. Just because they smiled didn't mean they liked him. Their smiles were painted on and fearful.

Melanie let go of the steering wheel, reached over the passenger's seat, and popped open the door. "Get in!"

The girls scrambled inside, filling the space beside and behind her. Infectious she-clowns or frightened stowaways? Melanie couldn't tell. The Beetle veered onto a nameless path. Pines towered to either side in a thick black curtain, their needle-coated branches grasping at streetlights.

The Cadillac rumbled alongside. Did he ever stop grinning? *Just my sunny disposition*, his teeth assured her.

Café girls clustered around Melanie, pawing and curious. She focused ahead. This way dipped deeper into the woods. Beyond headlights and luminous streets stretched a dark road. No more streetlights; only blackness lurked here.

Cadillac stuttering, her admirer raised an eyebrow. *You sure you want to do this? Absolutely positive?*

She wasn't, but she cranked up the radio and floored the gas. None of her escapes had been sure things, every flight a flirtation with disaster. But this time, she wasn't alone.

Maybe that mattered.

Both cars sped onto the unlit road, where trees and sky fused into solid night. Melanie's radio blasted static, and the

Beetle's engine screamed. She and the café girls screamed with it, their smiles cracking apart. Deeper darkness reached for the oncoming cars, too absolute for headlights to pierce.

Too absolute for him. His engine yelped, tires skidded, and he U-turned with his Cadillac's tailpipe between his legs. His music faded with him.

Melanie kept driving until black woods smothered all light, where the Beetle could finally stop. There was no rearview mirror to check; the café girls were only shallow, panicked breaths in the dark. Melanie couldn't even see herself.

She stepped out of the Beetle and onto soft soil, where unseen creatures slept and crawled. They did not insist she join them, only invited. She and the café girls were free to lie here or to walk back to the world where the Cadillac roamed.

Melanie stretched herself across cold earth, amid trailing fingers and teeth that broke her skin and chilled her blood. One café girl sprawled beside her, and then another, until each lay in the blackness. Their breath, and the breath of the things around them, synchronized and became one. Music of the darkness, the departed.

Right now, Melanie could take anything but him.

Recitation of the First Feeding

I never told my parents about the ghost girl.

From a young age, they expected me to sleep through the night in my own bed. Children's nightmares weren't their problem, no matter what stories Grandmother told when we'd gather at her place on days off from school. If anything, those story-filled summers on her porch and winters by her fire assured me nothing bad would happen so long as I heeded her warnings. Don't read a book that promises gold; don't take ice cream from smiling strangers.

But the ghost girl was no story. Some nights I'd lie in bed waiting for sleep, but instead her shape would wash across my bumblebee-patterned nightlight. There were nights she'd kick my toys, and others she'd aimlessly wander the house.

There were nights she'd climb into my bed. I'd wake up to her chill across my back, her face in my hair, and we'd stare into the bedroom's darkness together.

People can get used to anything. In time I realized she wouldn't hurt me, not in an obvious way. We lay side by side in bed, her thinking whatever ghosts think while I wondered why she was there. She sometimes mimed me when I sipped water or scratched my head, but other nights I followed her lead, wandering the house without purpose, never sleepwalking but not always in control.

Especially when she got me in trouble.

My little sister's plastic dolly wound up in my room. She'd spent the better part of a day searching, only for our father to find it under my bed. He shook it at me like an accusation—*Why is my daughter's dolly in my son's room?*—but didn't say a word.

My mother's nail polish was worse. My parents started giving me looks, and I overheard them at night discussing aloud what might be wrong with me, if I liked boys, and I didn't understand. Was I supposed to hate boys? I didn't want to hate anyone. Eyeliner, leggings, and lipstick all turned up in my room, even my mother's lace and silver cross. I might've thought that was fine, but my father said it was a bracelet, unfit for me to wear.

Not once did I mention the ghost girl. I was in enough trouble without looking loony.

The overheard conversations piled up between my parents and teachers, the principal, other parents. Whispers swirled at school about things I didn't understand. What did I do? Why did everyone suddenly hate me?

It was the ghost. She wanted to live and would do it through me if she had to. Her spectral fingers slid my mother's belongings under my pillow, and the nights I mimicked her, didn't I use them? I tried to be puppeteer and not puppet, but the line was blurring between us. If I let this go on, I would end up possessed.

Grandmother knew stories about possession. She knew stories about worse things than ghosts. To absolve myself these sins of makeup and jewelry, I would need worse things.

The ghost girl had to go.

When the summer solstice freed me from sixth grade that year, I left home in the early morning and started uphill toward Grandmother's house. My friends would soon be gathering downtown at the roller rink or arcade, places kids were allowed amid Briarstead's stores and hotels, but I had grown-up work to attend. Here and there, dirt trails shot off into a wilderness of woods and ponds. Where town's edge plateaued, the trees gave ground to golden fields of grain, wheat, and grazing cows. Briarstead was an odd hodgepodge of fertile rural and urban landscapes.

Grandmother's one-floor wooden house and the property where it grew sat at the edge of one dirt trail. Yellow-green grass swayed to either side of the house, broken by islands of car tires and similar junk up to where the land hit the woods. The trees didn't encroach on Grandmother's property; her roots ran too deep.

She sat on the high porch in her wooden rocking chair, looking to the road like she knew I was coming. Wind snatched at her curling white hair and amber pooled behind her cataracts. She didn't look like me, my sister, any of us. Most likely we weren't related to her by blood.

"Morning, Alex," she said. "Sister coming? Friends?"

I shook my head. No one visited Grandmother alone, but we never understood why. A pitcher of lemon tea sat on a wooden stool beside her, ice cubes bobbing at the top. On summer days, we ran wild together across her property and then collapsed on her porch to soak up a story and cool drink.

"Don't suppose you're here for a story?" she asked. "Come on."

I stomped up the porch steps and sat on the highest. Grandmother stuck a slender glass of lemon tea into my hand. If only I could've sat there for the rest of my life. No need to be rid of the ghost girl if I never had to see her again. But then, I felt her with me, as if she'd followed from home.

I turned to Grandmother. "I need to know more about the court that eats."

Grandmother's ancient mouth curled into a stern, knowing smile. "You don't want their help." She rocked back and forth. "We call them the Culinary Court. Most things like them don't make much of names, but they'll take what we give. The right setting, they'll come. They'll eat."

"Where?" I asked.

"Highland. Visit those hills with the court in mind and the table will be waiting, but you'll have to bring dishes, cutlery, and food. Don't call them without bringing something they'll want to eat. Set the meal in courses, and etiquette will chain the court. Once that's run dry, you'd best get going until their next feeding. And the next." Grandmother's rocking chair paused. "Once you start feeding them, it's on you to keep feeding them. They always come back, you hear? Best be sure."

I was sure. Probably the people in her stories were sure, too.

Grandmother stood, and skirts unfolded in layers around her husky legs. "I'll lend you the silver setting." She opened her groaning screen door, let it crash behind her, and returned with a sagging brown backpack. "Heavier than it looks."

I glanced inside at silver dishes, forks, knives, and spoons.

"Return every piece." Grandmother zipped the hefty backpack shut and slung it around my shoulders. "Last warning. Bring nothing you can't bear seeing eaten. Desperate summoners craving the court's help, they bring things that they want eaten, or things that stand for what they want eaten, but they forget to leave behind what they mean to keep. Don't make that mistake. If you love it, leave it someplace else. Not a favorite hat, a pet, not even thoughts on those you love. Only what they'll want to eat and what you're willing to feed."

I thanked her. She ruffled my hair and wished me luck.

Farther along the woods, golden flatland grew green and hilly. Even on its highest mound, you couldn't see any houses, only the thick trees of Briar Woods most seasons, the Kanawauke Pond through naked branches in winter, and the black suggestion of Appalachian Mountains year-round. It's the quietest place I've ever been.

"Only the wind lives in Highland year-round," Grandmother once told me, an earlier summer. "It's a place of meetings and partings. Never stay the night."

If there were a real place where Grandmother's stories might take place, it was Highland. Summer people gathered there for music festivals, but in autumn you got the sense that other things traveled through, and in winter, kids said you could hear babies crying in the surrounding Briar Woods. Spring rains washed the hauntings out, again made it a place for mortals in summertime.

But summer could be a time for other things, too.

I set my mind on the court and walked until the grass became a dry ocean. It had been a clear day, but the sky darkened as I neared Highland's center, forecasting rain that never fell.

I spotted the table nestled in a green dip with slopes on all sides. Its glass surface reflected the blackening sky. Six high-backed, ornate chairs surrounded it, one on each end, two at each side. I slid down the grassy dip and unzipped the backpack. Grandmother had packed six sets. The sky danced in their silver.

There was clockwork to setting the table, and I was a clumsy eleven-year-old. Each time I set a dish a little off from its chair or placed a knife on the wrong side, I packed it all up and started again. This wasn't family dinner table setting where I laid each plate and then tossed lumps of silverware to either side. I needed etiquette. We didn't have much of it in Briarstead, but it was all that chained the Culinary Court.

I began again at the end of the table and worked place by place toward its head.

It was midday when I finished. Wind swirled above the dip, but not down the slopes, perhaps afraid to upset the table. If Grandmother's stories about the court were true, they had power to eat those gusts and leave Highland's winds still and dead.

A bell rang over the hills, and the land rumbled as if a thunderclap ripped through the earth. The court had arrived.

Six pale horses slowed to a canter at the lip of the grassy slope, their manes dark as the sky, and turned to one side, revealing the bone-white carriage they drew. Gold trim lined its windows where the gloom hid the passengers inside, but I made out five shapes. On a splashboard atop the carriage sat a coachman in a brown patchwork suit and stunted top hat. He tugged the reins until the horses came to a full-stop and then slipped alongside the carriage toward the door. We never spoke. I was too scared, and when his dry face flashed an open-lipped smile, he showed neither teeth nor tongue. His gloved hand, the fingers poking free, grasped a gold ring on the carriage door and swept to one side, opening it.

Grandmother should've told me what to do with my hands. I fished a folded piece of paper from my pocket and clasped it behind my back. Sweating in T-shirt and jeans, I probably looked silly. Surely the Culinary Court had seen worse.

They had eaten worse.

I knew their names from Grandmother's stories. The Starvation Artist clambered out first. He was a skeletal creature, bones tied loosely together by dry skin that stretched from his distended gut. His eyes were sewn shut. Long fingers and toes picked through the grass, down the slope toward the table. Despite his name, he ate as much as the one that slithered behind him.

My heart sank when I laid eyes on the nightmarish Glutton, a white segmented creature, like a worm and a maggot mixed together, whose face was thorny teeth and whose six sapphire eyes shined from each side of its serpentine head. Wet, fingerless limbs helped it down the grass. I doubted it had any use for utensils.

"Bonjour," it croaked. Its toothy face rippled, but I couldn't read its expression.

Those first two turned my stomach, but the rest chilled my blood.

The Connoisseur crept next from the carriage doorway. Unlike the first two, he clothed himself in a pale violet, double-layered jacket, its white frills puffing from the chest and sleeves. His slender pants rolled down to his knees, where white socks tucked up underneath. Black shoes crunched the dry grass, their silver buckles agleam. He was pale as the horses, blue veins drawing faint maps beneath his skin, and a white, curling wig crowned his head. His tiny mouth was sewn shut, the flesh around the thread scarred white. He treaded down the slope, bowed to me, and stood to one side. His violet gaze never left me.

The Scholar emerged next, who I first mistook for a he since her clothes copied the Connoisseur's. Charcoal hair slicked back along her head. Jet black shades hid her eyes, almost always perusing the enormous hardbacked book that she slung open across one arm. Her other arm held a quill ready to strike the pages. She descended behind the Connoisseur.

"Name," she said.

I swallowed hard. "Alex."

"Alexandra."

"Alex." I paused. What was she asking? Had she mistaken me for a girl like I'd mistaken her for a man?

"My mistake." She said it like a curse. Her pen snapped across the page the way my teacher would mark a failed exam. Was it rude to have corrected her and I'd risked breaking etiquette? "The First Feeding by the Summoner Alex."

Last came the Gentleman. He dressed same as the Connoisseur and Scholar, but his arms and legs stretched much longer. His spindly body prowled down the slope, where he clasped his hands beneath his chin. He had no hair, eyes, nose, or ears, his flesh long ago burned and scarred white. A lipless, tar-gummed mouth peeled open, where pointed tigerfish teeth were too happy to see me.

"Bonjour, bonjour!" he almost sang. "The Culinary Court has not graced this land in some time. I do not suppose French is spoken fluently yet in Highland?"

I shook my head.

The Gentleman's grin deepened. "Pardon. We did not intend for our voiture à cheval to frighten. If we might begin?" He clapped his hands.

The coachman scurried downhill and began seating the court in the order they had appeared.

I offered my piece of paper to the Gentleman in trembling hands, afraid he might nip my fingers. The paper was folded like a private note passed in class. This one held my worst secrets, all about the ghost girl and what I needed from the court to be done with her.

"Ah, la carte." The Gentleman unfolded the note, peered eyeless at it, and handed it to the Scholar.

"Two of the summoner's courses." She spread it over one side of her ledger. "I will transcribe it before we begin."

"Merci, mon amie." The Gentleman watched the coachman seat the Scholar and then started toward the head of the table.

An impulsive urge hit me to put the court's horrible faces out of my head. I fought the words out of my mouth, a request that would haunt me long after the meal's conclusion. "There'll be one last course, but I didn't write it down."

The Gentleman turned. "Oh? Dessert?"

I turned from the gaze of his teeth, each point glaring at me. "I'm not sure you can eat it."

The Scholar flipped pages. "We dine fine on wars and worlds. We have savored tiny morsels of love and swallowed species whole. Our palettes have tasted dreams and dragons and the final unicorn, flavors now lost to eternity."

The Glutton sighed, forlorn. The Connoisseur offered a stitched smirk.

"It is all in the preparation," the Gentleman said as he clasped his hands and leaned over me. "S'il vous plait. What does the summoner bring to the table?"

From his seat, the Starvation Artist's long fingers scraped the glass surface and made it shriek. "Tell us. Bring us. Give us."

The Gentleman glanced back, the corner of his mouth curling in annoyance.

If he hadn't turned those awful teeth from me, maybe I'd have kept quiet. "Eat my memory from now until it's over," I said. "I don't want to remember what you do to—" I almost said *to her*, but I chinned at the paper I'd handed over, where I'd written what I wanted the court to eat.

The Gentleman answered with a revived grin. Behind him at the table, the Scholar's quill chewed at paper.

From what I could tell, the meal began at that moment, but everything from my sitting down to their carriage rolling again across Highland—that was an empty chasm in my head.

And my heart. The court left a hollowness growing beyond memory, telling me that the purging of the ghost girl was not an exorcism. It was crueler, colder, and cut my insides like no stranger's amputation should. Had I known her before she haunted me, some dead sister whose existence my parents had kept a secret? Just who had I fed to the court? There was no telling; that gap in my memory was complete.

I thought that last request would ensure an ordinary life, unscarred by that dark day.

I was wrong.

Grandmother's warning rang true. "Once you start feeding them, it's on you to keep feeding them."

Weeks passed between some meals, months between others, but the Culinary Court always came back, and they came hungry. I fed them my hobbies, fascinations, fondness of others, and guilt. All flavors of life, thrown onto their table and down their throats. Their constant return never let me forget that there was a feeding I'd forgotten, a ghost girl now digested. I couldn't remember the meal itself, but I knew it had happened.

Worse, not only did I feed them scraps of my past and personality, but my future. Every feeding took a precious piece of me, and with it went all its possibilities, skinned from time and served on silver dishes.

Cut enough pieces from yourself and soon you'll have nothing to give. Once I became nothing, I would have nothing to give, and then what would they eat?

When I turned eighteen, I abandoned Briarstead.

"Let them starve," I told myself. Doubtful they would, but I didn't care.

Four hundred miles away, I found work as an orderly at a drug clinic. Meds to carry, papers to fill out, supplying nurses when they had sutures to sew and snip, it went on as things do.

Mae Starling and I met there and soon moved in together. I can't say I brought a personality to the home we made together, but she wasn't looking for more than someone to help share life's burdens. Even incomplete, I could do that.

I thought little of Briarstead, and sometimes I even forgot the ghost girl. My childhood home seemed more ghost than she was, especially after my father called to say they were selling it.

"At a loss, but better off than some," he said. Briarstead was dying. Crops were failing, businesses were closing down, and property values were dropping.

Not my problem, I told myself. Life with Mae went on. Our biggest trouble was deciding whether to adopt a kitten or rescue a grown cat, and when we couldn't decide, we'd put off the whole thing for the umpteenth time.

But I couldn't run forever. The ghost girl was gone, yet on the quietest nights, she haunted my dreams. I'd wake gasping, soaked in sweat, and expect to find her with me. She had become disconnected from Briarstead, but her memory remained attached to me, almost alive. I'd gone to Grandmother's that summer solstice to rid myself of the ghost, and succeeded, but had it been that simple, she wouldn't have haunted me decades on. I should've been glad she wasn't clinging to me at night, taking my sister's things, worming her way inside my soul. Instead, everything had felt wrong ever since.

Something else had happened at that First Feeding. It ate at me decades later, much as the court had eaten the ghost girl, because I couldn't remember it. Memory is a kind of haunting, ghost or not, and the absence of memory can haunt, too, a word forever at the tip of the tongue, a face always familiar yet never known.

One quiet night, Mae stirred in her sleep beside me and then sat up. Wavy blond strands clung to her heart-shaped face. "You're still awake, Alex?" she asked. "Another nightmare?"

"Just dreams," I said.

She thrust her head onto her pillow and stared at a ceiling too dark to see. "Same here. I dreamed we adopted a cat after all, but then forgot her in the basement, so she ate our boxes, the floor, atoms, abstract concepts. And she wasn't a little cat anymore, but a panther. I think she hated me. Then I woke up."

I shuddered. "What do you think that means?"

"Sometimes forgetting to feed a thing doesn't mean it starves." Mae smiled sleepily. She had no idea how she'd splayed my worries on the sheets between us as if spread across the court's damn table. "What did you dream?"

I reminded her she had an early shift at the clinic and waited to hear her snoring.

I then climbed out of bed, got dressed, and wrote her a note saying I got a call from my parents, needed to head home and help with some things, that I hoped to be back soon. If I didn't come back, I didn't want there to have been no goodbye. That wouldn't be fair. We were never close the way some couples become, but she was good to me, and maybe she could say the same. I'd hoped to marry her someday, but that hope was small, and I took it with me in my pocket when I started my long, despondent drive.

Briarstead welcomed me just after dawn.

Steel shutters and out-of-business signs covered storefronts with unfamiliar names. The roller rink had been replaced by a hardware store that likewise went under, and the arcade had been demolished. Every hotel bore a Vacancy sign. Summer people might still have glutted the town for music festivals, but that would do little to help the year-round woes. Potholes scarred the road that led past my childhood home. It didn't look like anyone lived there, and certainly no one was left to haunt it but me.

Abandoned farmland rolled on, and beyond that lay the dirt trail to Grandmother's house. I parked at the property's weedy edge and approached the porch steps. There was no rationale for believing Grandmother still lived, but there she sat in her creaky wooden rocking chair, smiling her creaky wooden smile. She either hadn't aged a day or was so old that decades made no difference. A new oaken cane leaned beside her rocking chair, and the wooden stool had been replaced by a proper table, but the pitcher of lemon tea sweated eternal. It might as well have been that summer solstice morning.

"Alex," she said. "Grown a bit."

"Yes, Grandmother."

"Left quite a mess behind, you did." Her smile widened. "Come on."

I stomped up the steps and sat in a fold-out patio chair beside her. It didn't feel right, but I was too old for the top porch step. She poured me a glass of lemon tea. It seemed almost a contract, that there would be no strange talk until I drank her special brew.

"You recall the court, don't you?" she asked.

I nodded, gulping tea.

"Then get what you came here for. The silver ain't been moved."

I set down the glass and fetched the backpack that still kept six sets of silver dishes and utensils. "Have they always been five?" I asked. "Never more or less?"

Grandmother scoffed. "How old do you think I am? Their origin's before my time. I learn the stories, child, and then I pass their warnings along. Of course, some can't listen."

"Do you know the story of their first summoning?" I asked. All the past feedings were bothering me, and I'd noticed a detail I hadn't when I was young. I needed clarity.

Grandmother leaned back, and I almost felt my little sister and our childhood friends surround me. "In this part of the world, at least. It was a family feud between two farmers. One of them carried the story of the court from his homeland and summoned them to Briarstead, set them eating his rival's crop like a famine. The feedings went on until he had nothing left, and then the court ate him, too. Best hope your time in the world has given you more to feed them than the skin off your back."

"And did the Connoisseur eat then?" An idea was coming together. Time would tell if I'd survive it.

Grandmother's face wrinkled in a scowl. "I don't truck with details, child." She had that luxury; I didn't. She poured me another glass of tea for the road. "Need a reminder for how you go about this summoning?"

That part I hadn't forgotten.

My fingers were far less nimble than when I was eleven, but even then my first try took hours. As feedings went on, I had setting the table down to a science, placing two forks on the left and working to the right, setting the dish, two knives, and two spoons. My hands remembered, simple as riding a bike. You never forget, no matter how much you want to.

No matter what else is forgotten.

When all other places were set, I laid the forks at the head of the table. I was in no mood to make careless mistakes and dance this dance for hours. Mine was a simple request. "Give me back the last course of the First Feeding," I whispered, practicing bravery. The last silver dish clacked beside the forks.

At the First Feeding, I'd brought them a scrap of lined paper from my marble notebook. This time, I brought only my words. I supposed it was fair that I had to say this aloud. I'd had to say the last thing aloud when I was eleven, the thing I came to undo. I set the knives and spoons at the head seat with a heavy clink.

Thunderous hooves trampled grass above. The carriage appeared at the slope, no different than decades before, where the coachman released the Culinary Court.

Nothing had changed. Even though I'd grown, the Gentleman still towered over me, the Connoisseur's lips remained bound, the Glutton's sapphire eyes shined, the Starvation Artist crawled, and the Scholar stared from behind her black shades. Did she suspect anything about my return? I couldn't guess what secrets she kept.

I cleared my throat. "Give me back the last course of the First Feeding."

They gathered behind the Gentleman and bellowed their answer in unison, everyone but the Connoisseur. "We do not retch. We do not return. We eat."

My knees buckled, but I wouldn't cower. I wasn't a child anymore. "Can't you at least tell me what happened?" I asked. "It wasn't a simple meal, and you keep a history."

That seemed to settle the tension. Even the sky relaxed. "A Recitation of the First Feeding," the Scholar said, fingers drumming her ledger's thick cover. "With permission."

I faced the Gentleman's carcharodont grin. He clasped his hands beneath his chin and tilted his scarred head. "Let us discuss it over le repas," he said. "Show us what you bring to the table."

The Culinary Court's friendly act was part of their game. They had the power here. It was their privilege to show mercy or cruelty. Only the rules of their game kept me from becoming the meal.

I had to play.

The coachman hurried to seat first his masters and then me at the table's end, across from the Gentleman at the head. A hard chair, but I settled into it.

The game of the Culinary Court is played in symbols. Since the First Feeding, I'd brought an old yoyo so they could eat my kindergarten bliss, my late German shepherd Moxie's collar so they could eat my fondness for her, and on it went until I'd abandoned Briarstead to its fate.

"You've been eating the town," I said, reaching into my jeans pocket.

The Glutton preened at the Gentleman's side. "A fattened town."

"Manners, Monsieur Glutton," the Gentleman said. "Highland is pledged to our feeding so long as you are summoner. So, too, Briarstead has fed us its prosperity. It was not yours to serve, but we've made meals of it nonetheless in your absence."

If I fed them what was mine, I reasoned I might help those shuttered storefronts and crumbling streets. My hand slipped out of my pocket and placed my cell phone at the center of the table.

The Starvation Artist to my left slid pointed fingers across my arm. "What gives? What brings?"

The glowing screen showed the last call I'd made to my father. "The first course is my pride," I said. "Pride for having overcome my parents, left Briarstead, moved on with my life."

I took a fork and knife, their silver freezing my fingers, and sliced the phone apart. At the court's table, cutlery carves anything, even concepts. I passed plastic and LED chunks to each dish, where they twisted into braised chicken encircled by mushrooms, onions, and garlic in a pond of red wine.

I eased back behind an empty plate. My purpose was not to eat. The Connoisseur to my right was the same, though he had a full plate to sniff and prod and never taste. I couldn't smell the food, only what grassy odor floated at the table's edge.

The Gentleman tasted first. "A complex dish. The meat is rich in vain accomplishment, but glazed with aged anxiety, each vegetable grown in a garden of failure. Worthy of a final course, yet curiously served first. Magnifique."

The Scholar scribbled the Gentleman's observations, took a modest bite, and then jotted down her own. Food vanished noisily from the Glutton's and Starvation Artist's dishes. The Connoisseur drew a handkerchief from one coat pocket and patted his pasty forehead, his wrists nearly bony as the Starvation Artist's.

"I worry about him," I said. "When has he last eaten?"

"Ages ago," the Scholar said, drifting through her ledger's pages. "The Connoisseur last snipped open his lips at the Feast of the Final Unicorn."

The Connoisseur's eyes aimed at the sky in dreamy reminiscence. He probably held the flavor on his tongue, unwilling to part with it until a superior meal came along. Nothing I'd given had ever graced those sewn lips.

"I wonder what would change his mind," I said. "Has the court ever dined on one of its own?"

The Scholar adjusted her shades. "That would set a terminal precedent and catalyze the end of the Culinary Court."

"But if he's waiting for something exceptional as a unicorn, wouldn't court members qualify? How can one be a member if they won't eat?" I leaned toward the Glutton. "Something unique that he could savor, to restore himself."

The Glutton clacked strange teeth.

"You've become quite the conversationalist," the Gentleman said. "Perhaps that loquacious demeanor will be the final course."

He observed right; before, I'd only been court's dutiful servant who announced their courses and sat in silence while they ate. Now, I had ideas.

I reached back into my pocket. "There's a second course to come before the end."

My hand slipped across the table and laid a white gold ring on the glass, its band glittering with tiny shards of cubic zirconium. An inexpensive engagement ring, less than Mae deserved, but when I bought it, I'd thought she would appreciate the money saved.

"My love for Mae Starling, who might've become my fiancée." A silver blade carved through gold. Once placed on dishes, the ring's pieces transformed into mounds of black chocolate and oozing milky cream.

The Gentleman, as always, took the first bite. "No love tastes sweeter than love lost. The regret has a thick, pleasant texture that slides gently between tongue and palette. Mae Starling was special." I wondered how he knew lost love so well, what sort of person he might have been before he joined the court.

Mae had always deserved better, but I'd long ago fed the best parts of myself to these fiends. With that love devoured, I hoped to free her from someone who was never going to pop the question. She might meet a lover capable of deciding about a cat, or a baby.

I kept that to myself. If the court knew that the second course benefited a third party, they might have snubbed the meal. They might have questioned what I was up to.

As before, the Scholar tasted and wrote, the Glutton and Starvation Artist inhaled their food, and the second course mounted the first on the Connoisseur's plate. I wanted to shake him for wasting such a precious meal, but I didn't.

I had other plans. "What happened at the First Feeding?"

"Patience, s'il vous plaît," the Gentleman said.

"We agreed to talk about it over the meal. This is the second course. If we wait through the third course, it will be after the meal and out of line with our agreement." And more to the point, I needed to know before my plan came to fruition.

The Glutton rose from its seat and spat. "Do you know who we are? You witness disciples to great digestion everlasting. We follow the absolute feasting of the cosmos, great universal maws that devour galaxies and time and light. What little presence you are is not a morsel, not a crumb, to the vast stretches of—"

The Gentleman grabbed the Glutton by the throat and hauled it up to his teeth. "Your manners, Monsieur Glutton. Find them before you're excused from the table." He let go, and the Glutton sulked in its seat, six eyes drilling an ashamed stare into its dish.

The veil had dropped for a blink and revealed the court's true selves, volatile creatures of obsession and threadbare rules, the game showing off its players. They would tear each other apart outside their joint fixation. Etiquette alone chained them.

"For your patience, summoner, merci." The Gentleman waved a hand to the Scholar. "Mon amie, if you have finished dining on the second course, feel free to recite to our host."

The Scholar set down her fork and flipped pages again, never consulting any table of contents. The book was well-read, a part of her. Her finger found her place.

I gripped the table, and its harsh glass edge dug into my fingers. The gap in my life was about to fill. I didn't expect it would make up for the many feedings since, every piece of myself I'd sliced apart on this table over the years, or the damage done to Briarstead since I'd left, but I would know why the ghost girl still haunted my dreams long after she was gone. At least, I hoped. If this couldn't bring closure, at least there was the final course.

But no matter what, I had to know.

"A Recitation of the First Feeding." The Scholar cleared her throat. "The young summoner, Alex, offered our first and second courses in writing and the last spoken aloud. Alex sat in the summoner's seat and knew not court etiquette. Being so young, we guided him in serving us and hoped for etiquette to sharpen over subsequent feedings.

"The first course was the deeds done by one that Alex called the 'ghost girl,' Alexandra, so that all actions on her part would be annulled in the eyes of friends, family, and peers. A letter to us was transcribed, cut apart, and served to the court. The Gentleman considered it a slim yet enjoyably tart confection, its sauce a sweet raspberry of youthful confusion. I found its texture solemn.

"The second course was Alexandra herself. This came most difficult as Alex neither prepared a symbol nor understood what this demanded. We depended upon the Starvation Artist's precise fingers to pry open the child's throat, from which the court pulled this avatar of inner self onto the table. Alex could not bear to serve her and spent the course shaking and weeping. As no member of the court should sully their refined hands, our good coachman helped tear Alex's manifested inner self asunder so it might be served. The Gentleman described a rich, meaty meal, basted in resentment and yet strengthened by it; earnest seasoning drawn deep from the summoner. Rare does a summoner offer so core a piece of their insides. On this course I tasted confusion peppered with longing.

"For the third and final course, the memory of the first two courses was taken from the summoner. This required the Glutton to go on eating memory until the rest of us were finished so that every piece pertaining to the meal itself was gone, per the summoner's request. The Gentleman found it anticlimactic, with too much of the previous dishes' flavors to have unique appeal, yet still worthwhile for the creamy remorse at its center. I agreed that this was the most savory point yet did not agree on its being anticlimactic. This course held the only awareness of what the summoner had done and its ramifications wrought upon the rest of the summoner's life."

The Scholar turned the page, nodded, and flipped to where she had left off with the present meal.

I dropped my head into my hands, wanted to scream, couldn't. Grandmother had tried to warn me that no good ever came from asking for help from dark powers. Lying in bed in the dark, I'd wondered why the ghost girl made me take things and worried that she would soon possess me. But she was already inside. My life had felt hollow since the First Feeding because a crucial piece was missing.

Manifested inner self.

There was never a ghost. She was an imaginative explanation for why I'd taken interest in my sister's and mother's things, why I wanted to be less like my father and more like them. There was a girl inside me, trying to wake up.

And I'd fed her to these things. Now I understood why the Scholar called me that name when we first met. What had seemed like her misunderstanding was mine, my mind misled by parental expectations and the presence of unfortunate elements of my anatomy. Without all that mortal drudgery, the Scholar had known the truth. She'd seen through to me better than I'd seen myself.

Alexandra.

I looked to the court, all eyes and mouths staring. "I was her," I said. "That part of myself, you let me think she was a ghost trying to possess me. But that was me inside, and you didn't say a thing. We carried on with the meal." I was shaking by then, my absent personality at last giving way to barely contained rage. "You ate my soul."

"Spirit and future, a surprising course," the Scholar said. Between us, the Connoisseur again patted his forehead.

"None of your meals have been quite so filling," the Gentleman said. "Premature talentueux."

My fingertips squeaked the table's glass. "Can't it be undone? A trade?"

Every mouth roared open except the Connoisseur's stitched lips. "We do not retch. We do not return. We eat."

The Gentleman clasped his hands, but now his teeth threatened through a grimace. "Revenons à nos moutons. The third course, summoner."

"The third course." Tight-lipped, I smiled.

Grandmother's stories of the Culinary Court, like the one about the farmer, said that when the summoner had nothing left to offer at feedings, the summoner became the last course. That was a natural consequence to summoning the court. Some circle-of-life universal rhythm dictated that, after getting what was wanted and then losing everything, the summoner who fed would be eaten. I was not oblivious to this.

But I'd kept my eye to my right through this meal, teasing out what I needed to know, goading their thoughts by my questions. The Gentleman had figured me right— quite the conversationalist this time. Still, he hadn't figured why. I had no intentions that any more parts of me be eaten, not again, no matter what I had to do.

Goodbye, Mae.

"At your pleasure, Gentleman." My right hand slid around the icy unused knife beside my dish. My left hand found the fork with longer prongs. "It's delicate, sifted out of countless others. One of a kind."

The Glutton chuckled, its pale skin shimmering and oily. I faced it, as if I meant to lunge across the table, but the corner of my eye lingered to my right, where the Connoisseur leaned closer, intrigued.

My knife slashed at his lips, splitting the sutures open. My fork dove behind the blade, impaled his purple tongue, and the blade swung back, slicing it free. It wriggled on the prongs, a living thing itself, as the Connoisseur's mouth gushed crimson slobber.

"The third course is the Connoisseur," I said. "A meal like no other." I didn't wait for the table to transform his tongue, just stuffed it into my mouth. It slithered past my lips, licked my tongue, and trembled down my throat. I didn't have the refined palette or culinary language to describe the flavor, but I would've likely agreed with the ledger entry for the Feast of the Final Unicorn.

The Gentleman's jaw dropped, razor teeth parting. The Connoisseur groped at his mouth with his handkerchief. Blood poured down his white frills.

The Scholar realized she had pressed her quill to the ledger and was making an ink blot. She drew it back. "We cannot," she said. "Remember, this would set a terminal precedent."

"Because the court would cannibalize itself, but why should he be part of the Culinary Court when he doesn't eat?" I asked, and licked my lips. "Or when he won't share the last flavor of the unicorn?"

The Glutton's sapphire eyes blinked envious emeralds. Beside it, the Starvation Artist pawed at the table, found a drop of the Connoisseur's blood, and licked it off one finger.

Inside me, the tongue was changing. I was changing. I hadn't expected that, but I should have. The court had tainted Highland and Briarstead; why should I be excused? Since the First Feeding, I'd been another Briarstead landmark boasting a Vacancy sign. Now the tongue flowed through the empty space that the ghost girl had left behind, across limbs and blood vessels, lungs and intestines. My clothes burst, reformed, and took on new shapes.

"You can't eat your own," I said. "Fine. Cast out the Connoisseur and I'll replace him."

They looked to each other. If I hadn't been so distracted by the sharp cramps through my organs, I might have better observed the war across the table between etiquette and novelty, the game against unity.

But there is neither honor among thieves nor unity at great feasts, and the unicorn's flavor was too enticing.

The Gentleman chuckled behind one hand. I pictured his teeth bared in that laugh, but for the first time it didn't unnerve me. "C'est la vie," he said, and waved his hand to one side.

The Scholar turned her ledger to its first page. "The Connoisseur is expelled, and in his stead, we welcome—" Her quill tore across ancient paper. "—the Countess."

The Connoisseur gaped at her, but he had no tongue between his bloodstained teeth. It had reached every avenue inside me.

The Gentleman clapped his hands. "The third course."

I grabbed the Connoisseur by his stuffed shirt and hauled him onto the table. The glass showed me a grand lady, writhing hair black as the sky, neck crested by white spines, her black dress flowing with violet frills, before the final course's blood drowned my reflection. I tore the Connoisseur apart bare-handed, the way the coachman had torn my soul, and served him to each member of the court. He became soft piles of stewed venison, drowning in spices and rich wine. For the first time, my dish was full.

The Gentleman took the first bite. "Lean, as one would expect, but brimming with secret, forgotten flavors. He kept much of the old days to himself. I taste unicorn, dragon, the ancient peoples who once roamed the horizon between sky and sea. Footnote, include references to those appropriate final meals." His grinned at me. "Mademoiselle, merci beaucoup. Your final course is a delicacy."

The Scholar paused her writing to wipe at dark tears that leaked beneath her shades. She added nothing after the Gentleman's assessment, only savoring another bite. Even the Glutton and the Starvation Artist took their time. They felt nostalgia that I couldn't share; the Connoisseur hadn't dined on my soul.

Still, new strength grew inside me. The ghost girl was gone, buried by rejection even from herself, but I would live instead as this new thing, more like her than the haunted husk I'd been these past decades, and now ascended beyond mortality. My tongue stretched longer than my knife and savored the thick juices of the Connoisseur's remains.

"We must revise our rules so as to never permit this again," the Scholar said.

The grinning Gentleman reached over his dish and opened his palms toward me in a gesture of invitation. "Here we were called to recite the First Feeding of a summoner, and here we depart upon the First Feeding for the Countess. We welcome her to the Culinary Court. Je n'en crois pas mes yeux."

Whatever he'd said made the Glutton and the Scholar laugh. When the meal was finished, we left the table. The Starvation Artist clambered up the hill, where the coachman awaited beside the carriage's open door, followed by the Glutton.

The Scholar ascended after them, eyes on her ledger. "So many amendments to make."

For the first time in centuries, the Culinary Court had transformed. Grandmother's story and the Scholar's ledger would need revisions, striking out the Connoisseur's name while my new moniker swept in on a tide of ink and blood. Summoners would have to adjust the name on their tongues and please a fresh palette.

They would learn.

The sky began to clear, and the table faded into the wind. At the slope beneath the carriage, the Gentleman offered a spindly elbow. "To another meal."

"Already?" I asked, slipping a hand around his hooked arm. My voice came haughty and sure of itself, another change. I liked it.

His free hand fluttered as he led me uphill. "Mademoiselle, your appetite will need adjusting. We are the Culinary Court and travel all manner of places. Wherever there is one to serve their happiness salted with their misery, we are there to feed. If they are found wanting, they become dessert."

"And what if I'm picky, like your former colleague?"

Tigerfish teeth shined as we reached the carriage. Its insides smelled of flowery perfume. "You may intend to never feast on mortal woes, flesh, and souls, but that is most what they offer," the Gentleman said. "Choice is not our desire. We taste the variance offered by the universe. Bon appétit."

The Gentleman's cold, delicate hands guided me through the carriage doorway, where I sat beside the Scholar. He joined the Glutton across from us, while the Starvation Artist crouched beside the window opposite the door. The coachman closed us inside.

The Scholar smiled at me. I watched her write, but much of it was in French. I would have time to learn, I supposed, and looked to the windy fields. The coachman snapped the reins, and the horses pulled our carriage from Briarstead Highland, chasing the black storm.

Grandmother would soon send someone to fetch her silver. Someday, I'd be back, months or years later, when she told the story of the Culinary Court to another desperate soul. I would've preferred not to hurt anyone. There were too many parasites in our little entourage.

But if our summoners only served misery, eventually I would have to eat. As time stretched onward and mortal lives became fragments against the breadth of my immortality, I couldn't be certain I would care about them forever. They might come to hate me.

And unlike when I conjured up my ghost girl, I didn't mind that threat of hate. I would devour hatred merrily and lick its juices from my sweet lips.

ACKNOWLEDGEMENTS

We can't properly credit the small synchronizations of the universe that sometimes lead us to the right places, but I want to at least thank the wonderful people who've worked so hard to help me.

Thank you to Sarah and Rob of The Seventh Terrace for taking in this collection of strangeness. Also thank you to Sarah for being an absolute pleasure to work with, especially helping to hone a particularly difficult new story to sharpness. I also want to thank the cover artist, Janice Blaine, for giving these anatomical elements a brilliant face to show the world.

To the past stories' editors, Sandra Ruttan, The Arcanist Team (Josh Hrala, Andie Fullmer, Patrick Morris), B.R. Sanders, Katy Lennon, Eddie Generous, and many more: Thank you for tending to my stories when they needed a hand and then giving them a place to stand and shout.

A special thanks to Laurel Hightower for lending her words to introduce mine. She has mastered the art of somehow ambushing me with trumpeting praise.

And largest and therefore impossible to name them all, the online horror community. I've formed so many precious friendships and sisterhoods in the strangest of places. All of your encouragement means the world, and I hear it in every passionate, guttural shriek we let out each night for ourselves and each other.

And to J, thank you for the home we are together. Wherever life will take us, if I'm with you, then I'm whole.

ABOUT THE AUTHOR

Hailey Piper is the author of *The Worm and His Kings*, *The Possession of Natalie Glasgow*, and *Benny Rose, the Cannibal King*. She is a member of the Horror Writers Association, and her short stories appear in *Year's Best Hardcore Horror*, *Daily Science Fiction*, *The Arcanist*, *Dark Matter Magazine*, *Flash Fiction Online*, and elsewhere. A trans woman from the haunted woods of New York, she now lives with her wife in Maryland, where they spend weekends summoning goat monsters and singing to the moon. Find Hailey on Twitter via @HaileyPiperSays or at her website, www.haileypiper.com.

PUBLICATION HISTORY

"Feast for Small Pieces" © 2019 Hailey Piper
Originally published in *The Bronzeville Bee*, reprinted in
Year's Best Hardcore Horror, Volume 5 by Red Room Press

"The Law of Conservation of Death" © 2019 Hailey Piper
Originally published in *The Bronzeville Bee*, reprinted in
Rigor Morbid: Lest Ye Become by Bronzeville Books

"Demons of Particular Taste" © 2020 Hailey Piper
Originally published in *The Arcanist*

"I'm Not a Chainsaw Kind of Girl, But…" © 2019 Hailey
Piper
Originally published in *Vulture Bones #7*

"Candyland" © 2020 Hailey Piper
Originally published in *Twisted Love* by Bronzeville Books

"Elf-Bride" © 2021 Hailey Piper
Published in this collection *Unfortunate Elements of My
Anatomy*

"Aggressive Mimicry" © 2019 Hailey Piper
Originally published in *Black Rainbow, Volume 1* by NBH
Publishing

"Seven Signs He Doesn't Love You" © 2019 Hailey Piper
Originally published in *The Macabre Museum #1*

"Crones in Their Larval State" © 2019 Hailey Piper
Originally published in *The Arcanist*

The Seventh Terrace

Visit us online at
www.the-seventh-terrace.com

ALSO AVAILABLE FROM
THE SEVENTH TERRACE

CPSIA information can be obtained
at www.ICGtesting.com
Printed in the USA
LVHW041806031022
729849LV00002B/345

9 781990 082017